DESSIE MARIE

Dessie Marie

BY JACK SNOW

Dedication

To my daughters, Mandy Snow, Jennifer Hire,
and Kathy Snow, who encourage and support me in all my
life's endeavors, I dedicate this novel. I wish them much love,
happiness, and success.

Dessie Marie
JACK SNOW

ISBN: 979-8-9859700-0-5

CONTENTS

PROLOGUE

I woke up early this morning and built a fire in the wood stove. These types of old-timey wood stoves have kept this house warm for seventy years. Hob and I moved into this four room house when we got married in 1927. I was a happy bride all of just nineteen years old, and Hob had just turned twenty.

This house was just a shed when we moved in. Hob worked throughout the years on our home, adding running water and even a small bathroom with a real small shower. As far as I know, our house was the first to have running water, much less a bathroom, on this old Brushy Mountain. Hob saved as much money as possible throughout all the years we were married. When he saved a thousand dollars or more, he would buy land that adjoined us. I asked Hob why we didn't spend more money on our house instead of land. Hob would just laugh and say, "Dessie, land is much more valuable than a house. God ain't making no more land."

Then I thought about my two cousins, Turkey Holler Bill and Lou, and my brother, Charlie, and wondered what a hardship it had been for them to live without even running water. Turkey Holler Bill and Sister Lou lived alone in shacks stuck way up in the steepest part of this old mountain. Charlie lived alone down by the New River. Turkey Holler Bill, Lou, and Charlie got their water from streams close by their shacks, and each had only an outhouse for a bathroom. It's been almost a year, but still not a day goes by that I don't think about them and their tragic deaths.

I was taken out of my thoughts by the smell of fatback grease getting hot in my old cast-iron skillet. As usual, I cooked myself a fried egg and a piece of fatback and made a slice of toast. When I finished my breakfast, I poured myself another cup of coffee and made my way onto the front porch to sit in my rocking chair and enjoy whatever peace came my way. *Winter will soon be here,* I thought as I watched the fall leaves blow across the yard. The poplar leaves looked like huge golden snowflakes falling around my old mountain home.

My thoughts were interrupted when I heard a vehicle slowly making its way up the mountain on the old graveled dirt road. I soon saw a shiny black car pull up to my mailbox and stop. A young lady with long blond hair opened the driver's door and headed up the path to my front porch. She waved as she got closer and said, "Are you Dessie Marie Pennell?"

I felt a little uneasy but simply answered, "Yes, and might I ask who you are?"

The beautiful young lady said, "My name is Mary Holder, and I work for the *Charlotte News.* I was assigned the task of writing about the Brushy Mountain murders that happened a while back."

"Well, ma'am, I don't know you, and I have never heard of the Charlotte News. Most people on this mountain are quiet, simple folks and keep to their self, and I sure don't want anyone knowing my business. So, if you would quietly leave me be, I have chores to do."

"I stopped down at the grocery store in Moravian Falls and asked the group of old farmers sitting around drinking Cokes about the murders. Each one told me that Dessie Pennell was the only one that knew the real story of the tragedies," Mary said. "I really need this story, Miss Dessie. I'm afraid I'll get fired if I go back without it. I'm three months pregnant and don't have any other financial support. Will you please reconsider?"

I looked into Mary's blue eyes and could tell by the tears and the expression on her face that she was serious. I thought, What the heck. *If Hob was here, he would tell the story. And besides, I don't want to do any chores today anyway.*

"Okay, Mary. I'll tell everything I know as best I can. When do you want to start?"

"Oh, thank you, Dessie," Mary said as she ran over and hugged me as if she was one of my younguns or something. "Let's start now. I brought notebooks in the backseat of the car. How about you getting us both a cup of coffee, and we can sit out on your porch so you can tell me everything you know? Make sure you tell everything and don't leave anything out. I'll be back in a split second, and we can begin."

I thought, How bold, but I already knew that I liked Mary and that she and I would get along just fine.

I soon returned to the front porch with two hot cups of black coffee and settled down in my rocking chair next to the anxious and excited young reporter.

Mary said, "Start wherever you like, Miss Dessie. I'm all ears, and I've got my notebooks and pens ready."

"I guess I'll start back when all the shenanigans and tragedies began just about this time last fall. I'll just tell it like it happened, and if you need me to stop or you need a break, just let me know, Mary."

CHAPTER ONE

It was a brisk and cool fall day when I was interrupted by my first cousin Lou beating on my door at six in the morning. Lou was better known on this old Brushy Mountain as "the Dog Lady." Lou had at least eleven dogs that lived with her in a shack on the side of Brushy Mountain near Moravian Falls, North Carolina. Her shack had a fireplace for heat, no electricity, and no running water. Lou got her water from a nearby stream and cooked in cast-iron pots and pans in a rock fireplace. She and her dogs slept on a mattress made from old feed sacks stuffed with straw. Her bed was located close to the fireplace for heat and close to the front door, where her firewood was stacked.

The dogs, mostly curs, were small and had short hair. Most, I think, were of a terrier breed mixed with beagles and other curs that lived throughout this mountain. Those eleven dogs were Lou's whole life, and she called them her children that she never had. Her favorite of all her pups was a dog she named Little Beaver. Little Beaver was a touch bigger that the rest of the pups and didn't ever let Lou out of her sight. Little Beaver was solid white with just a small black patch of hair on its short, stubby tail.

Lou's speech was impaired because of a lisp. However, she said her dogs understood everything she said. I, too, over the years adapted to Lou's speech and very seldom had to ask her to repeat what she said. Lou was dressed in overall jeans with a red and black ragged flannel shirt and a wool army overcoat. She wore what we called a toboggan hat, which most people called a stocking cap. Her boots were rubber, and she had bought them from a Sears catalog.

I greeted Lou at the door with a hot cup of black coffee and a big hug. When she stepped into the den and sat on the sofa, I noticed that her eyes were watery and red. I immediately asked, "Lou, what's wrong? You've been crying."

Lou began to cry harder as she told me that her sister, Ida, had been found dead in her old cabin yesterday evening. Ida, better known in the mountains as Turkey Holler Bill, was about the same age as me and lived as a hermit in a rotting-down cabin on top of Brushy Mountain. Turkey Holler Bill lived by herself since her husband took their daughter and fled to West Virginia under the pretense of seeking work in the coal mines. To my knowledge, she had never seen her daughter since but had spoken to her on the phone. Turkey Holler Bill told me that when she made her monthly walks to Moravian Falls for groceries, she would call her daughter from a pay phone at the grocery store. Her daughter's name was Hattie Mae. She was probably over sixty years old.

As I hugged Lou, I whispered that I was so sorry Turkey Holler Bill had passed and asked how she died and who discovered her body.

Lou was still crying when she softly said, "Just died of old age, I figure. Charlie discovered her when he made his monthly white lightning run, selling moonshine across the mountain. Charlie put Turkey Holler Bill in the back of his old black truck and hauled her off to the funeral parlor in Moravian."

Charlie was my twin brother and lived alone down by the New River. He made a living making and selling moonshine to just about all the folks living on this old Brushy Mountain. Problem was that Charlie liked drinking his moonshine as much or more than selling it.

Lou said, "I saved enough money over the years to give Turkey Holler Bill a proper burial down at the Baptist cemetery in Moravian Falls. I knew that saving my late husband's army pension would come in handy one day." She added, "I think that's the only good thing that sorry-ass husband of mine ever did for me or anyone else." She reached into the zipper pocket of her dirty overalls, pulled out a huge handful of hundred-dollar bills, and said, "I got a bunch more money in each of my rubber boots. I got so many bills that I had trouble walking down the mountain, especially through the apple orchard with its tall grass. Dessie, will you help me count it? You know I only made it through the third grade, and my counting ain't that good. Daddy made me quit school right before I turned nine. He said if I was old enough to go to school, then I was old enough to work in the apple orchards and the tobacco fields."

With that, Lou, still sitting on the couch, struggled pulling off the rubber boots filled with her dirty, sockless feet and hundred-dollar bills. She pulled the sweaty bills out of each boot and placed them on the coffee table, along with a crumpled piece of old newspaper with writing on it. The smell of old money, newspaper, and dirty feet quickly filled the room and my nose. I picked up the dirty bills and arranged them in stacks of five on the table. When I finished dividing the money, I had one bill left over.

"Lou, you have nine stacks of five, making your total forty-five hundred dollars. That's a lot of money," I said.

Lou giggled just a bit and said, "Don't forget the extra one that didn't fit into a stack. Dessie, how much do I have now?"

"That would make forty-six hundred total, Lou, more than enough to give Turkey Holler Bill a fine burial service," I said. "What's that written on this piece of newspaper?"

Lou started to tear up again. "That's the telephone number for Turkey Holler's daughter, Hattie Mae. Turkey Holler gave it to me years ago, just in case something bad happened to her.

When I walk down to the funeral parlor in Moravian, do you think old man Buford would punch the number in his phone, so I can tell Hattie Mae her mama is dead?"

"I'm sure he'll help you make the call to Hattie Mae, especially if you tell him you're going to pay cash for Turkey Holler's funeral. I'm sure he thinks he'll have to bury her and just take whatever money the state pays for burying poor people," I said. "Do you know where Hattie Mae lives? Maybe she can take a bus up here for her mama's funeral. I know that Turkey Holler Bill would like for her only child to come say a proper goodbye."

"I think I heard Turkey Holler say that Hattie lives in the mountains of North Georgia, somewhere around a little town called Helen," Lou answered. "I'll ask her when I call if she has enough money to take the bus up here and pay her last respects. She can stay at my house, so she'll need no money for a motel."

"I expect she's about sixty-three years old by now, since Turkey Holler had her when she was just sixteen," I said. "And as far as Hattie Mae staying at your house, that is totally out of the question. No way would anyone want to stay with all those dogs, and when the only heat you have is from that old rock fireplace." I thought, *I know I wouldn't sleep in that old shack with them dogs and the cold, not to mention Lou's cooking.*

As far as I knew, Lou only ate squirrels, rabbits, and small horny-head fish she caught from the nearby stream where she got water. In the fall, she also gathered apples from the orchard, and in the spring and summer, she picked wild blueberries and blackberries and mushrooms that grew on this old mountain. Years ago, Lou tried to raise a garden, but it just got washed away because the mountain where her shack stood was very steep. She did, however, manage to build a potato-planting bed by stacking two eight-foot-long logs on top of each other for the sides. Then she stacked two four-foot logs for the ends. When she finished, she had an eight-foot-by-four-foot rectangle approximately two feet deep, making her a sort of raised bed for potatoes. The mountain was so rocky that there was no use trying to fill her potato bed with dirt. Lou planted her patch by cutting her seed potatoes in half and placing them in the bottom of her raised bed with the eyes facing up. Then she simply raked leaves from around her shack and piled them on top of the seed potatoes. She then watered them in good by carrying buckets of water from the creek. When the potato plants began to grow, she would add more leaves to her bed. After the plants bloomed and Lou was hungry for potatoes, she would reach under the leaves, feeling for fresh potatoes and being extra careful not to harm the plants. She planted her bed in February and harvested potatoes until late fall.

Hob made us a garden when we moved into this old house.

He had a friend come with a big piece of equipment that scraped off the topsoil behind the house into a huge pile. Then he pushed dirt and mountain rocks around until he cleared off a level space about fifty feet by one hundred feet. He then placed the topsoil onto the level space, making a nice, big garden. Hob and I planted green beans, corn, potatoes, cabbages, lettuce, green peppers, and lots of tomatoes. Hob sold most of the tomatoes down at the local food store in Moravian Falls.

Lou interrupted my thoughts. "Well, if I'm going to the funeral home in Moravian, I best get to walking. It takes me at least four hours to walk down the mountain and five hours to walk back, because it's so steep. Dessie, if old man Buford gets Hattie Mae on the phone, I'll stop back by here and let you know what's went on about Hattie Mae and the burial and all."

I said, "Lou, you be careful walking down that old dirt road. Watch for cars and snakes, and I'll keep a watch out for you and leave the porch light on for you to return."

And with that, Lou stuffed the bills back into her rubber boots, pulled them on, got up from the sofa, and walked out onto the porch. I watched from the porch until she was out of sight and thought, *Lord, please walk with her and protect her.*

"Too much detail, Mary? Am I talking too fast? You haven't said a word since I started."

"No, no, Miss Dessie, you're doing just fine. I'm quiet so as not

to break your train of thought. And believe it or not, I'm able to write down word for word. Please continue," Mary said.

"Okay, let's see, where was I?" I said.

CHAPTER TWO

When Lou left, I went back into the house, thinking about Turkey Holler Bill and Lou and how we rarely got to see each other. Even though we were cousins, we rarely spent much time together growing up, or even when grown. Not many people that lived on this old mountain had cars or trucks. Most just walked everywhere they had to go. My husband, Hob, once had a truck he used to go to work down in Moravian Falls at the mirror factory. He worked there for several years and retired about ten years ago. Hob passed just a short two years after he retired. Lord knows I couldn't drive, and all my younguns were grown and raising families of their own, so I gave his old truck to my brother, Charlie. Charlie told me that in exchange for the truck, he would have a telephone put in this old house for emergencies, and that he would make the monthly payments.

Charlie used the truck to make deliveries of his moonshine to a lot of folks that lived throughout these mountains. Charlie made shine near all his adult life. Problem was, he enjoyed drinking it as much as selling it.

Story has it that one Saturday night way back in the Depression, Charlie was down by the New River making a fresh batch of moonshine when the urge hit him to drink some himself. It was cool out, and the fire from the still and the shine Charlie drank kept him warm but also made him so drunk that he passed out on the riverbank. The next morning when Charlie woke up, there was a long line of people standing down by the New River. Charlie thought, being that it was the Depression and all, someone had formed a soup line by the river, just like people did in town. He dusted himself off and got in line.

The next thing Charlie knew, this man grabbed him and dunked him under the water and quickly brought him back up. The man then asked Charlie, "Did you see Jesus?"

Charlie quickly answered, "No, I didn't."

So the man dunked Charlie back under the water and quickly stood him back up while asking, "Did you see Jesus this time?"

"No, no, I didn't," was Charlie's reply.

The man grabbed Charlie a third time and dunked him back under the water, holding him a little longer before bringing him back to the surface. The man then shouted, "Did you see Jesus?"

Charlie shouted back, "Are you sure this is where he fell in at?"

I spent the rest of the day cleaning up the kitchen and doing laundry while waiting to hear some news about poor old Turkey

Holler Bill and Hattie Mae. It was about four o'clock in the afternoon when I heard the sound of Charlie's beat-up pickup coming up the steep, dusty mountain road. I went to the front door and saw Charlie pull his truck right up in my front yard. I watched as he and Lou got out of the truck and stepped onto the flat granite rocks leading up to the porch.

As I opened the front door, Lou said, "Old man Buford got Hattie Mae on the phone, and when I told her about her mama, she just sobbed."

"Calm down, Lou. You and Charlie come in and sit while I put on a fresh pot of coffee, and you can tell us all about your phone call," I said.

I opened the front door wider for them to come in. When Charlie and Lou passed by me, I could smell a little shine on Charlie's clothes and breath. "I was just thinking about you, Charlie, before you and Lou got here," I said.

Charlie said, "Now, Dessie, I know what you were thinking, and they'll put your telephone in next week. I know it's been a while, but things are tight, and it took me a lot longer to save up the money than I thought. They'll be here first thing Monday morning to put in your new phone and show you how to use it. I was coming up the mountain to tell you about the phone when I passed Lou walking, so I stopped to give her and them dogs a lift." Charlie sat down with Lou on the sofa.

"Will y'all quit talking about the stupid phone? I need to tell you about Hattie Mae and Turkey Holler Bill's funeral arrangements," said Lou. "Old man Buford took the crumpled-up newspaper I had in my boot and dialed the number, then handed me the phone. That's when I told her about her mama. After Hattie had herself a good cry and was still sobbing, she asked how her mama died. I explained that she must have fell off a cliff near her house and died from the injuries, and that Charlie found her. I also told her that her mama was at the funeral parlor in town and that the director said we could take our time for the funeral service, to give her enough time to make arrangements to get here. Hattie told me that she retired from being a schoolteacher last year and that nothing would keep her away. She said that she had her own car and could be here by next Monday. I handed the phone back to old man Buford, and he gave Hattie the phone number to the motel in Moravian."

"Did you and old man Buford decide when Turkey Holler Bill will be buried, and where?" asked Charlie.

"We are going to bury Turkey Holler one week from today at the Baptist cemetery in town," Lou said. "That will be next Wednesday, the sixth day of September. One thing me and old man Buford couldn't figure out was how Turkey Holler's body got so bruised and bloodied up. She had a big gash on the side of her face, and her arms were scratched up and bloody. We guessed that she fell down one of them steep hills on the mountain, hurting herself bad, but was able to make it back to her cabin, where she died from her injuries."

"Yeah, she looked beat and bruised up pretty bad when I put her in the back of the truck," said Charlie. " 'Course, riding in my old truck bouncing down the mountain to the funeral parlor didn't help any."

"How did you find her?" I asked.

"I parked my truck down by her mailbox to deliver her monthly dose of shine as usual," said Charlie. "I hollered for her, but she never came out of her cabin. I started just to put the shine in the mailbox but then remembered I needed the extra cash. So I struggled and climbed up the hill next to her house and hollered for Turkey Holler again. She still didn't answer. I could see that her front door was open, and the screen door was partly closed. I knocked on the screen door and hollered her name again. That's when I saw Turkey Holler lying on the floor next to the door, face down. Her body was cold and stiff as a board, so I knew she had been dead for a long time."

I thought, *Poor old Turkey Holler Bill, died all alone and never had the chance to say goodbye to her family, especially her daughter, Hattie Mae.*

Lou said, "Dessie, here is Hattie Mae's number. When they

put your phone in Monday, will you call and tell her to come to your house after she checks in to the motel?" With that, Lou reached into her dirty, stinking boot and handed me that crumpled piece of newspaper with Hattie's number on it.

"I don't have much experience using telephones, but I'll try, Lou," I said.

"I'll make my way back here Monday to meet Hattie, and the three of us can visit a spell," said Lou. "Charlie, you load them dogs back into the truck and take me home. It's been one hell of a day."

Charlie did as he was told. He jumped up, chased down the dogs on my front porch, and carefully put them into the bed of his truck. When Charlie got the last dog loaded, he cranked the old truck and yelled, "Come on, Lou! They're all loaded."

Lou stood up from the couch and hugged me hard before making it out the front door. Once on the porch, she turned to me and said, "Dessie, me and my babies will see you Monday afternoon."

As I watched them drive out of my front yard and back onto that old mountain road, I thought, *Eleven dogs fussing on my porch, and Lou and Hattie Mae coming for a visit, not to mention the telephone man. Monday sure is going to be a busy day.*

CHAPTER THREE

I got up early the next morning, put on a pot of coffee, and made me some oatmeal for breakfast. I planned on spending my day cleaning up a bit and putting on pinto beans for supper. I had a head of cabbage to cut up and fry and some potatoes to stew, and I figured I would make a big cake of cornbread. I knew that what I couldn't finish for supper, Lou and Hattie Mae might finish eating when they arrived on Monday.

It was getting on up in the afternoon and the smell of cooked pintos was filling this old house when I heard a car or truck winding its way up the road. I went from the kitchen to the front door in anticipation of seeing Charlie's truck pulling into my yard. I opened the door and was surprised to see my new friend's truck parked down at my mailbox.

Mike Wall moved to Moravian Falls about a year ago. Mike had lived in Davie County, North Carolina, on a small farm. When he retired, he built a big cabin on the side of the mountain down by the creek. Mike was best friends with my son-in-law, Jack Poplin, and my youngest daughter, Bonnie. Jack and Mike grew up together and even worked together for many years. Mike said he moved here for peace and quiet, and that he had promised to build on the piece of mountain his grandpa had left him. Mike picked me up the morning of the first Monday of every month and took me to town to shop for groceries or whatever else I needed.

I opened the front door as Mike got out of the truck and headed for my porch. "Hey, Mike. It's not Monday. Is there anything wrong?" I said loudly. "Bonnie and Jack are okay, aren't they?"

As Mike was making his way to the front door, he waved and smiled to let me know everything was just fine.

"You scared me, Mike. I thought something must be wrong for you to visit on a Sunday," I said. "Come on in the house and I'll pour us a big glass of sweet tea." I opened the screen door and headed for the kitchen.

As I poured tea, Mike came in, sat on the lounge chair, and said, "Dessie, I just wanted to stop by and tell you how sorry I was to hear the news about your cousin dying. I was at the store in Moravian and heard the local farmers talking about her. They said she must have fallen off the mountain but was able to drag herself back to the house. They said she was bruised and beat up pretty bad."

"Yeah, that's what we figure happened, and that she must have died from internal injuries," I said. "It sure is nice of you to check on me." I handed him the glass of cold sweet tea.

"Lou, my sister, is going to have Turkey Holler Bill buried next Wednesday, down at the Baptist church."

Mike said, "Dessie, let me know what time, and I'll pick you and Lou up and take you to the funeral."

"That sure would be nice. I was already dreading trying to get into Charlie's old truck. Plus, I'm sure Charlie will have a drink or two before the funeral," I said. "Mike, I've got some good news. They're going to put me a new telephone in this old house Monday. I hope I can figure out how to use it."

Mike then got up, walked over to the coffee table, picked up a pen and notepad that I used for my grocery list, and wrote down several numbers. "The first number is my home number, and the second is Jack and Bonnie's number. When you get your phone installed, call me with your number and then call Bonnie. I'm sure she'll be thrilled to hear your voice," said Mike. "Well, I best be going. Oh, by the way, I got a visit from Sheriff Bobby Spillman and some other feller this morning. The other feller said he was from Independence, Ohio. It's a Northern town located on Lake Erie. He said that the sheriff was taking him around to meet folks in Moravian and on the mountain. He said that he's in the market to buy land and property and wanted to know if I might be interested in selling my place. Of course, I told him no, I was not interested. He said his name was Jim Clanton, and if I changed my mind to just get in touch with the sheriff, and he would stop back by. I didn't think too much of it and sent them on their way."

"Well, Mike, if Sheriff Bobby Spillman has anything to do with it, it can't be good. Sheriff Bobby is as crooked at a dog's hind leg," I said.

"It's getting late, and I best be going," Mike said.

Mike handed me his empty tea glass and was soon back in his truck and headed down the mountain to his beautiful cabin by the creek. We called that part of the creek the Noah Hole. That's where most baptisms took place.

CHAPTER FOUR

The next morning while I was cooking grits and eggs, I was startled by someone beating on my screen door. I looked out the window and saw a white van sitting down the road a piece. The van had a picture of a large black telephone on the side and the name Bell Service underneath. There were several large ladders on the top that stretched over the van's front window.

When I opened the front door, I was greeted by a tall, young, blond-headed boy dressed in the uniform of the phone company. "My name is Ty Copeland, and I'm here to install your new phone. Are you Miss Dessie Pennell?" he asked.

"Yes, I am, and I'm a little excited about the phone. Is it hard to use?" I asked, all in one big breath.

The young man reached into his work bag and handed me a new telephone wrapped in clear paper. "See the numbers on this keypad?" he asked. I nodded my head, and he said, "You just put the receiver to your ear and punch the numbers of the person you want to call. It's just that easy."

"Did you say your name is Copeland?" I asked. "Are you related to Tony and Earline Copeland that lives over on the other side of Moravian toward Wilkesboro?"

Ty replied, "Yes, they're my parents, and they still live on the north side of Moravian Falls near Wilkesboro. Dad retired a few years back, and now they just work around the house and garden."

"Your mom and dad used to come visit all the time a few years back," I said. "In early spring, Earline and I would sit on the front porch and drink coffee and talk while your dad would help Hob plant the garden. In the summer, Tony would come help Hob pick vegetables and even drove him to town to sell them to the local grocery store. In the winter, Tony would come hunt with Hob, shooting squirrels, rabbits, and occasionally a deer. Our freezer was always full of fresh mountain game."

"Well, Miss Dessie, in just a couple of hours, I'll have your new phone installed, and your first call can be to Mom and Dad," said Ty. "All I have to do is run a line from that junction box on that pole to your house." Ty pointed at a pole just down the road. "Then I'll install a phone jack on your wall, plug in the phone, and you'll be ready to go."

In about two hours, I made my first call from my new phone. Earline answered the phone in a sweet voice. "Hello."

"Earline, this is Dessie Pennell, and Ty just put in my new phone, and he suggested that I call you first," I said.

"What a pleasant surprise," said Earline. "Tony and I was sorry to hear about the death of your cousin, Turkey Holler Bill.

Tony and I will try to get up to visit with you after the funeral. We know you'll be busy for the next week or so."

We said our goodbyes as Ty gathered up his tools and headed back to his work truck. He waved goodbye and headed down the mountain toward town.

I remembered that I was supposed to call Hattie Mae and ask her to come by my house after she checked in to the hotel in Moravian Falls. I found the crumpled-up newspaper that Lou gave me and punched in the numbers written on it. I held the receiver up to my ear and listened while I heard two rings.

A lady answered the phone. "Hello," the sweet voice said.

"Is this Hattie Mae? This is Dessie Pennell, your mother's cousin, calling from the top of Brushy Mountain," I said. "Lou, your mama's sister, wanted me to call and ask you to come to my house after you check in to the hotel."

"Why, yes, this is Hattie Mae," she answered. "It's good to hear from you, Dessie. My mama told me a lot about you. I haven't seen my mama since I was just a little girl, but we talked on the phone every month when she made her trip to town for groceries. I always suggested to Mama that I drive up for a visit. Her answer was always no. She said she was ashamed of the way she lived, and her past."

I could tell by the quaver in her voice that Hattie Mae was

starting to cry. I changed the subject and said, "What time do you think you'll get here?"

"From Helen, Georgia, to Moravian Falls is just about a six-hour drive," said Hattie. "I was just about to leave when you called. I should be at your house by seven this evening. Dessie, can you give me directions to your house from Moravian Falls?"

"Just ask anyone at the hotel or the grocery, and they will gladly give directions to my old house on top of the mountain," I said. "I can't wait to meet you, Hattie Mae. Drive safe, and remember that all your family on top of this old mountain loves you."

I hung up the phone and remembered that Lou and Charlie would be coming as well, and that I should get busy straightening up and getting ready for company.

My thoughts were interrupted when there was a loud banging on my front door.

CHAPTER FIVE

"Sheriff Bobby Spillman here, Miss Dessie! Open the door so we can talk a spell," he yelled.

I slowly walked over to the front door and looked through the glass to see Sheriff Bobby Spillman and some other man. The other man was tall and skinny with blond hair and looked to be a rough character with all his tattoos. His hair looked oily and was combed straight back and parted down the middle.

As I opened the door, I said, "Sheriff Bobby, why, you never visit. Must be something real important or serious. Who is this fellow here with you, sheriff?"

"This man here is Mr. Jim Clanton from Independence, Ohio. Can we come in and visit for a spell?" Sheriff Bobby said, all in one breath.

"I'll just come out on the porch, and we can sit and talk there, if you don't mind, sheriff," I said.

"Sorry to hear about your cousin Turkey Holler Bill, Miss Dessie. I know you will miss her something terrible," Sheriff Bobby said.

Just then, the other man interrupted and said, "Look, my name is Jim Clanton, and I've come all the way down here to this godforsaken place to buy quite a bit of property on this mountain and in Moravian Falls. Several people in town have already agreed to sell, including old man Frazer that owns the grocery store and Mr. Brock that owns the motel and several acres at the foot of the mountain. Let's see here. According to my map, Miss Dessie, you own seventy-seven acres on the side of this apple orchard." He pointed at the apple trees across the road in front of my house. "I'm here to pay top dollar, and you can move down toward Winston-Salem or to Georgia and live and visit with your daughters. So, what do you say, Dessie? Give me a price for this scrap of land and this run-down house."

"How did you know I have folks in Winston and in Georgia?" I asked while staring at Sheriff Bobby. "My place is not for sale, not now and not ever, especially to some slick man from Ohio. Now, you two get off my property so I can get back to my business."

The two men turned and walked toward the sheriff's car, parked down by my mailbox. Then the man from Ohio turned and yelled to me, "Dessie, I will own this land eventually, I promise! If you don't sell it to me, I'll buy it from one of your kids when you're dead and gone. Should you change your mind, just get in touch with Sheriff Bobby. He knows where to find me." Jim Clanton had a smile on his face.

I watched them head down the old, dusty road toward town

and thought, *What kind of men get pleasure trying to scare old people? I then went back into the house, thinking, I'll be seeing those two scoundrels again.*

I went into my bedroom closet, searching for Hob's 20-gauge shotgun. It didn't take but a second to locate it behind some of my winter coats. I had given Hob that old Ithaca pump shotgun for a present on our first Christmas together. I thought, *I wonder how many squirrels, rabbits, and quail, not to mention coons and possums, this old gun has killed.* Now I might have to use it on bigger game. I checked to make sure the gun was loaded and placed it on the floor under my bed for quick retrieval, if needed.

I went back to the kitchen and figured I would make some oatmeal cookies for Lou, Charlie, and Hattie Mae. Ever since I could remember, Charlie always loved fresh-baked oatmeal cookies. You could bet that if any were left, they would be going home with Charlie.

I had already put the last of yesterday's pintos on the stove and was also going to fix some fresh cornbread, stir-fried squash and onions, and fresh turnip greens for supper. I knew that Lou and Charlie would be expecting to eat when they came to visit with Hattie Mae. What I didn't know was if Hattie Mae liked country cooking, or if she was used to a finer side of eating.

It was getting on about six o'clock when the first batch of

oatmeal cookies came out of the oven. I was placing the cookies on top of the oven when I heard Charlie's old truck pull up in my front yard and park next to the porch. I slowly made my way to the front door to see him getting out of the beat-up pickup. As Lou got out, her dogs jumped out the back and onto my front porch—all except Little Beaver. When Lou and Charlie stepped onto the porch, I could see that Little Beaver was snuggled up in Lou's arms, covered by her old army coat.

CHAPTER SIX

When Charlie and Lou came through the front door and into the house, the first thing Charlie said was, "I smell oatmeal cookies and country cooking."

Lou said, "Dessie, never mind Charlie. Have you talked to Hattie Mae, and is she coming here?" She then pulled off her old wool army coat, wrapped Little Beaver in it, and placed it on the sofa. Lou sat down beside Little Beaver, waiting for me to answer.

I told Lou and Charlie that shortly after my phone was installed, I had in fact talked to Hattie Mae, and that she should be here around seven that evening. I then told them about my visit from Sheriff Bobby Spillman and that feller from Ohio.

Charlie said, "What did that crooked sheriff Bobby want?"

Before I could answer, Lou interrupted and said, "Yeah, they came to my place just after two o'clock, mumbling something about buying up my place. That feller from up north said he wanted to buy my shack and all 252 acres that my late husband left me."

"Yeah, I heard from several folks on the mountain that Sheriff Bobby and this city slicker was visiting and talking about buying up property," said Charlie.

Lou said, "I just showed them my old double-barrel shotgun and told them to get the hell off of my property and never come back. That feller from up north said he would be back in a few days to see if I had changed my mind. I just pointed my shotgun and aimed it over their heads, and then they both skedaddled back down the mountain."

Charlie said, "Lou, I bet that will be the last you see of them two."

Charlie was interrupted by the sound of someone driving up the mountain road and stopping in front of my house. It was getting dark outside, but I could see Mike getting out of his truck and heading up to my front door.

Charlie said, "That looks like Mike Wall. I wonder what he's doing here this late in the evening. I bet he could smell them oatmeal cookies and this country supper all the way down to his cabin by the creek." He opened the front door to let Mike in.

"Lord, Miss Dessie, I smelled cookies baking when I walked up onto the front porch," said Mike.

"Mike, come on in and have a cup of coffee and my famous oatmeal cookies," I said. "Maybe you can stay for supper."

Mike said, "No thanks, Dessie. I just finished supper, but I'll take a couple of cookies home with me. I just stopped by to tell you that Sheriff Bobby Spillman and Mr. Clanton came by my place again today, asking if I had changed my mind. Mr. Clanton said that they had visited you and that you were considering selling. I just wanted to stop by and check on you, Miss Dessie, to make sure you're okay."

"Them dirty scoundrels! I told them no, I am not selling, and to kindly leave me be. That's when that feller from up north got huffy and said he would buy my place either from me or from my children when I'm dead and gone," I explained.

Mike said, "I did a little research on Independence, Ohio, and found out that it's the home of one of the oldest amusement parks in the United States. It has over a dozen roller coasters, along with a ton of other rides. It even has a mile-long beach and water parks as well. I tried to find some information about Mr. Jim Clanton, but I turned up nothing on him. My guess is that Mr. Clanton is trying to buy up all the property in Moravian Falls as well as on Brushy Mountain to develop into a huge amusement complex. It's not a bad idea. This mountain is absolutely beautiful, and Moravian is such a quaint little town. It's close to Charlotte, Winston-Salem, and Greensboro, making it an ideal location for an amusement park, along with small retail shops and restaurants."

Charlie spoke up and said, "Dessie, you best be careful with Bobby Spillman snooping around. Don't many folks on this mountain care for him, and they trust him about as far as they could throw him."

Looking out the window, Lou said, "Well, here comes another car up the mountain."

It was almost dark as the car came to a stop behind Mike's truck. When she opened the car door, I could see that it had to be Hattie Mae. She was thin and tall, just like her mother, and even walked like Turkey Holler as she approached my front door. I opened the door and shouted her name. Hattie Mae smiled with tears rolling down her beautiful face, hugged me tight, and said, "Oh, Miss Dessie!"

An instant love fell upon me, Charlie, and Lou as Hattie Mae hugged and introduced herself to her newfound family.

Mike introduced himself to Hattie Mae and said, "Well, I best be going. It was sure nice meeting you, Miss Hattie, and I'm extremely sorry for your loss of your mom. Miss Dessie, you stay safe. You have my telephone number in case them two give you any more trouble."

Everyone said their goodbyes to Mike while Hattie Mae was getting comfortable on my old sofa.

"How do you take your coffee, Hattie?" I asked as I made my way into the kitchen.

"I'll just have water, Miss Dessie. If I drink coffee this late in the day, I'll be up all night," said Hattie.

I poured Hattie a big glass of cold water, wrapped up a couple of oatmeal cookies, headed back to the sofa, and sat down beside her.

Hattie still had tears in her eyes when I handed her the cookies and simply said, "Thank you."

Lou said, "You look just like your mama. You're beautiful, and Little Beaver says so, too." She pointed to her dog.

Charlie and I could tell that Hattie didn't understand anything Lou said because of her lisp. Charlie then spoke up. "Lou said you're beautiful and look just like your mama."

I asked Hattie if she would be able to stay for supper. She smiled and said that she had already eaten on the road from her house to Moravian Falls.

We spent the next hour or so talking about Turkey Holler Bill and things we had done together growing up. There really wasn't much to tell because we only got to visit with each other's family at funerals or sometimes at Christmas.

"Well, y'all, it's getting late. I only have a couple of days before we lay Mama to rest, and I still have to find someone or some company to auction her things and land," said Hattie.

"Auction?" asked Charlie.

"Yes. Mama always told me that upon her death, she wanted everything she owned actioned off, and the money to go to me in an effort to make up for all the years apart," said Hattie. "Miss Dessie, if I come and pick you up in the morning, will you go with me to town to finish all the arrangements about Mama's place and things?"

"It will be my honor," I said as I hugged her.

Charlie and Lou headed for the door with Little Beaver following close on Lou's heels. "Charlie, be careful loading my babies in the back," Lou said while she and Little Beaver got in the truck. Charlie got in, fired up the old truck, and drove up the mountain road toward Lou's shack.

Hattie came onto the front porch, waved goodbye to Charlie and Lou, and hugged me one more time. "See you early in the morning, Miss Dessie," she said. "I love you, even though we've just met. Seems like I've known you all my life."

It was only just a minute when I saw Hattie's taillights slowly going down the mountain road. I thought, *What a beautiful lady. I love you, too, Hattie.*

"Mary, for a reporter, you sure are quiet. Do we need to take a break?" I asked my new friend.

"You're doing great, Miss Dessie, but I could use a bathroom break and another cup of coffee, if you don't mind," Mary replied.

Soon, Mary was back on the porch. "Please continue, Miss Dessie," she said.

CHAPTER SEVEN

I got up early the next morning and put on a pot of coffee and cooked a batch of cat-head biscuits. I was preparing to make sausage gravy in my old cast-iron skillet when Hattie knocked on the front door. I cut the stove down to low and headed for the door.

When Hattie Mae got into the house, she hugged me tight and said, "Dessie, I can't believe that I'm going to bury my mama. I haven't seen her since I was six years old, and she never sent me pictures. I don't even know what she looked like." She started to cry.

"Hattie, your mother had a hard life, trying to live all alone on this old, rugged mountain. Turkey Holler Bill was a proud lady and never depended on anybody for anything. When you bury your mother, just remember all the monthly phone calls and stories y'all shared over the years. I know that Turkey Holler would be proud of you and all that you've accomplished." I poured her a cup of coffee, handed her a plate from the counter, and said, "Now, Hattie, dry them beautiful eyes and enjoy this great country breakfast I fixed just for you."

After Hattie loaded her plate with gravy and biscuits, she took a seat at my kitchen table and said, "We have an appointment at Nationwide Auction in Wilkesboro at ten o'clock. I made the appointment with Mr. Michael Langford, who said he was the owner."

"Oh, yeah, I know Mr. Langford," I said. "He is a fine, good-looking young man with a great reputation around these parts. Michael has auctioned off lots of property for folks, mostly to settle estates. I've heard he also does a great job selling personal items such as antiques and family heirloom jewelry."

"Mr. Langford said that after we meet and discuss his fees, he would take us in his four-wheel-drive truck up to Mama's shack to take an inventory of what items I want to sell," said Hattie. "He also said that he knows everyone in Wilkes County that is in the market for land, as Mama probably didn't have anything in her shack that anyone would want. He claims that he could make a few phone calls and have a big crowd of cash buyers there by Saturday afternoon."

When we finished breakfast, Hattie said, "Miss Dessie, let me help you clean up the kitchen and wash the dishes."

I told Hattie that the dishes would be there when I got back, and that if we had to be at Mr. Langford's office by ten, we should probably get a move on.

Soon, we were in Hattie's car and slowly making our way down the mountain. As we drove that old road, I pointed out all the houses and folks that lived on the side of Brushy Mountain.

The first house we drove by belonged to my closest neighbor, Preacher Wright. Preacher Wright built his home about fifteen years ago. Folks said that he was originally from the mountains of Tennessee, where he had made his living raising and selling pigs. He was a great neighbor that kept to himself but was always there if need be. When Hob passed, Preacher Wright was the first visitor I had, bringing food and offering any help that I might need.

Next, we approached Ken and Shelby Martin's place. Ken and Shelby lived in a huge two-story farmhouse with lots of outbuildings surrounding it. Most all the outbuildings stored farming equipment used for work in the apple orchards. Ken and Shelby owned nearly eight hundred acres of orchards on Brushy Mountain, as well as the Apple Co-op in Moravian Falls. Behind their house and outbuildings was about a ten-acre lake that was fed by a clear, beautiful spring that descended from the very top of the mountain.

The next house we passed was the home of Miss April Brandon. It was a small white house that was nestled into the side of the mountain with no backyard and a very small front yard. Miss April raised chickens for eggs and for meat. The chickens free-ranged around her yard and on the mountain behind her house. She would gather eggs every morning and afternoon. She sold her eggs to folks throughout these hills for a dollar and a half per dozen, and after her hens quit laying, Miss April sold them for three dollars each. Every Monday on our way home from grocery shopping, Mike Wall would stop by Miss April's and buy two dozen eggs for him and two dozen for me. He never let me pay not one cent for the eggs.

We were at least three-fourths of the way down Brushy Mountain when we passed by old man Billy Barr's place. He lived in a small, run-down trailer down the right side of the mountain. His trailer was much lower than the road that we were on. It looked like if a car ran off the road, it would land right on top of him.

"Listen to me good, Miss Hattie," I said. "Don't ever have anything to do with that mean Billy Barr. He has had run-ins with just about everybody living on the mountain. He came to my house shortly after Hob died and asked if I was going to sell my place. When I told him no, Billy Barr got real upset and said that Hob and he were the best of friends. He claimed Hob promised him that when he died, I would sell him my house and land. He said that the whole mountain was once his mom and dad's, and that everyone living on the mountain cheated them out of their land, and that he was going to get it back, no matter what. Rumor has it that he poisoned his first wife to death and that he locked up his second wife in the bedroom and cut off the heat. He claimed that he left her home alone to go on a week-long hunting trip and when he returned, he found her froze to death in the bedroom."

"Oh, no, that's horrible," said Hattie.

"Mind my words, Hattie. That man is of the devil, and you should stay far away from him," I warned.

Next, we were at the base of the mountain nearing the Noah Hole, where Mike Wall had built his cabin. Mike had a beautiful place real close to the creek and the Noah Hole. This was a beautiful natural scene. When you sat on Mike's front porch, the sounds of the creek water flowing over the rocks was mighty peaceful.

"This is where Mike Wall lives," I said. "You met Mr. Mike at my house the other evening. Mike is good friends with my son-in-law, Jack Poplin, that lives in Mocksville. They grew up together and even worked together for many years. Mike's grandpa deeded him that piece of land, and Mike promised that he would build a cabin on it after he retired. He comes up to my place the first Monday of every month to see if I need anything and to take me shopping for groceries."

"Mike seemed like a really nice man, and I'm sure you're glad that he checks in on you every so often," said Hattie.

Soon, we pulled into the parking lot of Mr. Langford's office and parked right in front, facing the door. His office was a small white-brick building with a dark gray metal roof. There was a big bay window in the front of the building with Nationwide Auction painted on it. Underneath the sign and in smaller white letters was painted, Michael Langford, Owner.

When we started to get out of the car, the front door of the office building opened and Mr. Langford quickly approached us, all the while waving. "I'm looking forward to helping you, ladies. Come inside and make yourselves comfortable in our conference room," he said.

Mr. Langford led us down a hallway and into a big office that had a large conference table with survey maps everywhere and a coffee pot on one end.

"Ladies, please have a seat," he said. "Miss Dessie, it's been a while, and you haven't changed a bit."

"Thank you. This is my cousin's daughter, Hattie," I said.

"Mr. Langford, my name is Hattie Mae, and my mother was Ida Brock, or Turkey Holler Bill, as she was known on the mountain. As we discussed on the phone, I want to talk with you about auctioning her land and all her belongings," Hattie said.

"Well, first off, please call me Michael, and I'm very sorry for the loss of your mother," said Michael. "I have pulled a survey map of your mama's place that also has a plot drawing of the approximate location of the home. This map shows that your mama owned eighty-one and a half acres close to the top of Brushy Mountain. Her property adjoins Frail Jones's property, which also has the fire tower lookout on it. Your mama's land has thirty-eight feet of road frontage and several small mountain streams. The name of the old gravel road going by it is Pores Knob."

"How soon do you think you could arrange an auction for Mama's place, as well as everything in her home?" asked Hattie Mae.

"Miss Hattie, I could put flyers out all over town as early as tomorrow, as well as placing a big ad in the Wilkes Journal, which comes out every Friday," said Michael. "In addition, I will have my staff call all our previous buyers in Wilkes County, Yadkin County, and Davie County, as well as Forsyth County. We can have a big crowd at the auction by as early as this Saturday afternoon."

Hattie said, "How much is all this going to cost me, Mr. Langford—I mean Michael?"

"Hattie, I generally charge six percent of all personal items sold, such as furniture, dishes, jewelry, and such," explained Michael. "For the land and the homeplace, my fee will be ten percent of the gross amount of the sale."

"Neither you nor I know what is inside my mama's old house, but what do you think the land will bring at the auction?" asked Hattie.

"Where your mama's land is located is mighty rough terrain," said Michael. "Driving up Pores Knob is not a problem. However, driving from the road to your mama's home and touring the land requires a four-wheel-drive vehicle. The folks that live on the mountain don't have a lot of money, so l would not expect a local buyer. The clients that I will invite from Wilkes and the surrounding counties will be able to pay cash, which affects the price somewhat. I think if you get six hundred dollars an acre, you'll be lucky."

Hattie said, "Mr. Michael, you're the expert, and if Miss Dessie trusts you, then so do I."

"Great. I'll get the contract ready for you to sign, along with an estimate of the gross sale, minus my fee, and the approximate net amount of your proceeds," explained Michael.

Soon, we were in Michael's pickup winding our way up Pores Knob toward Turkey Holler Bill's place. It had been several years since I visited Turkey Holler, and I could only imagine what we might find in that old shack of hers. Then I thought, *Hattie's insides must be busting. This is as close as she's been to her mama since she was six years old.*

CHAPTER EIGHT

Finally, we got almost to the top of Brushy Mountain and stopped at a falling-down mailbox on the side of the road. Turkey Holler Bill's shack was off in the distance, partially hidden by overgrown bushes and weeds. From the mailbox leading to the shack was a small path that Turkey Holler had made to retrieve her mail.

Michael said, "Ladies, while you're exploring the house and the contents, I'm going to take this survey map and drive the property and try to find the cornerstones. I'll meet you back at the house when I get finished."

As Hattie and I got out of the truck and headed up the steep path to the house, I could already see the tears welling up in her eyes. The closer we got, the more tears flowed down Hattie's cheeks. I squeezed her hand as we walked and tried to reassure her that everything would be all right.

Still holding tightly to her hand, I opened the front door of the shack, and we stepped inside. After my eyes adjusted to the dim light in the living room, I said, "Hattie, as I recall, your mama kept oil lamps throughout the house. I'll find one so you'll be able to see all your mama's precious things."

I walked into the kitchen, which had light coming in

through the window over the sink, and found an antique oil lamp sitting on the counter. Beside the lamp was a large box of kitchen matches used to light the old wood stove in Turkey Holler's kitchen. I lit the oil lamp, turned up the wick, and walked back to the front room. When I got there, Hattie had located an identical oil lamp sitting on the sofa table and was looking for matches. I handed her the lit lamp, took the one she had found, and lit it. With both lamps now glowing, the whole room was bright as sunshine.

"Oh, it's beautiful! Look how neat and clean everything is," Hattie said as more tears began to flow.

In the front room were a small loveseat sofa, a straight-back chair, a sofa table, and a small end table placed between the sofa and chair. Underneath the end table were a few magazines and Ida's Holy Bible.

Hattie slowly picked up the Bible, held it close to her chest with her eyes closed, and whispered, "Oh, Mama, even though we haven't been together since I was six years old, I have never stopped loving you."

Hattie opened the cover to the first page. Printed at the top of the page was

HOLY BIBLE

PRESENTED TO

In bold handwriting below that was "To my sweet baby, Hattie Mae, from your loving mother, Ida James."

At the bottom of the cover page was printed,

YOUR WORD IS A LAMP TO MY FEET AND A LIGHT TO MY PATH

Psalm 119:105

Hattie opened the Bible to where there was a long velvet bookmark at Psalm 23. "The Lord is my shepherd," she whispered as she cried softly, holding the Bible close.

On the last page of the Bible, Hattie found a picture of a little girl wearing a white dress with a blue hat. On the back of the picture, Ida had written, "My sweet Hattie Mae."

Hattie smiled and said, "Dessie, that picture was taken the week before my daddy took me to West Virginia. Mama kept it all these years. She must have truly loved me."

I took Hattie by the hand and hugged her tight. Together, we made our way through the small kitchen. Once we were in Ida's bedroom, we had to hold the oil lamps higher to get more light into the room. I made my way over to the window and opened the old curtains, letting in more light. The bedroom was small, with a twin bed neatly made and positioned just under the window. Directly in front of the bed was a large dresser with a mirror attached. There was a white jewelry box neatly placed in the center of the dresser.

Hattie set her oil lamp on the dresser and slowly opened the beautiful jewelry box. I moved closer, holding my lamp so she would have more light. Like a child at Christmas, Hattie pulled out every piece of jewelry and carefully laid them on the dresser.

"Look, Miss Dessie, it's Mama's wedding rings," she said as she slipped them over her finger and held up her hand.

Within the jewelry box were several antique pieces, including two necklaces and three or four bracelets. While Hattie and I were admiring the jewelry, we didn't notice that Michael had made his way into the house to the entrance of the bedroom.

"Michael, you scared me half to death! We didn't hear you come in," shouted Hattie.

Michael said, "I'm sorry, Hattie. I knocked, but y'all must have not heard me. That makes two of us that was scared half to death today. I was on the top of the property looking for a cornerstone when I heard a rustling of leaves behind me. I turned around to find a shotgun pointed right at my face."

"Oh, my Lord, are you all right?" asked Hattie.

"I'm fine, just a little shaken up," said Michael. "It was Frail

Jones. He owns the property that adjoins your mama's, that has a fire tower on it. Frail wanted to know why I was snooping around on his property. I told him that I was looking for the cornerstone on the property line because you're going to auction off the home and land this Saturday."

"Frail Jones is a hateful old cuss," I said. "Another one you best stay clear of, Hattie."

"Yes, I agree," said Michael. "Hattie, Frail was mumbling something about how he was cheated out of your place years ago by your daddy, playing poker at Charlie's moonshine still. He seemed pretty upset and let cusswords fly like it was going to change the situation. I told Frail that it was his lucky day, and he could buy this place back this Saturday afternoon. That made him madder than a wet hornet." Michael laughed.

"That's terrible. I don't think my father would have cheated anybody out of anything," said Hattie.

"Oh, just forget it, Hattie. That old coot don't know his butt from third base," I said.

Hattie changed the subject and said, "Michael, I have decided to auction off everything in one piece—the land, the house, and everything in it. I have all I want to keep for myself here in my hands." She held her Bible and jewelry box tightly.

"Well, in that case, it makes the auction a whole lot easier," said Michael. "Since you're going to sell everything at one time, it means I won't have to inventory and tag everything in the house or what's in the shed out back. One sale and one buyer."

"There's a shed out back?" asked Hattie.

"Yes, it's just up the hill a little way," said Michael. "Part of the tin roof is about to come off, but other than that, it looks stable enough. Do you and Dessie want to go take a look-see?"

Hattie Mae took me by the hand and said, "You lead the way, Michael."

We walked out the back door of the house and into an overgrown yard full of weeds and briars. Once we got to the shed, I could see that the door had fallen off and was lying on the ground. The old shed was only about ten feet wide and approximately twelve feet long. Hattie moved slowly into the shed while Michael and I stood just outside of the opening.

Hattie called out, "Not much in here, just a shovel, a hoe, a cane fishing pole with a bobber still attached, and a small trunk. I'm going to drag the trunk outside and let Michael open it, just in case there is something inside that will bite."

Michael bent down over the trunk, unlatched the hinge bolt on the front, and opened the lid. Inside were several *Alfred Hitchcock* magazines, along with other murder and detective books dating all the way back to 1956.

Hattie just smiled and said, "I'm ready to go now, if y'all are."

Soon, we were in Michael's truck headed back toward Wilkesboro. Michael said, "Miss Hattie, since you're selling everything at one time and I don't have to inventory all the furniture and stuff, I think it's only fair to reduce my fee to eight percent."

"See, Hattie, I told you that Michael Langford is a good, honest man and that he would treat you fairly," I said.

"I had no doubt, Dessie. Saturday can't come quick enough, so I can get all this behind me," said Hattie.

It was only a short ride. In no time, we arrived in the parking lot of Nationwide Auction. Michael opened the truck door and helped me to Hattie's car.

On the way back to my home, Hattie and I didn't say much, as I'm sure she was reflecting on the events of the day and thinking about her mother, Ida—or, as we knew her, Turkey Holler Bill.

It didn't take long before we were back on the mountain road heading to my home. I wasn't paying much attention while we drove along. I was too busy admiring the apple orchards that grew on the side of this old mountain.

I was startled when Hattie said loudly, "Who is that man sitting on your front porch?"

CHAPTER NINE

"**W**ell, I'll be," I said. "Why, that's my old friend Hamp. I haven't seen him in over a year. If you leave my back door and head straight past my garden and go about a mile and a half down the mountain, you'll find Hamp's old shack. There is a long dirt road that leads from the main highway to Hamp's place, but you have to have four-wheel drive to get there."

"He looks huge and mighty rough to me, Dessie. I'm glad y'all are friends," laughed Hattie.

"He's just a big teddy bear," I said. "He moved here about ten years ago, when he was released straight out of prison for murder. Hamp told me that he lived and worked in Detroit city. He was born and raised there and made a good living as a barber."

"Murder?" asked Hattie.

"Hamp claims that he got into a fight in a bar over a beautiful girl that worked there," I said. "He says a drunk guy was being abusive to the young lady waiting tables. Hamp says this drunk grabbed her and forced her onto his lap and wrapped his arms and hands around her and fondled her breast. Hamp got the girl free and with one blow knocked the drunk man completely out."

"And the guy later died?" asked Hattie.

"After knocking the guy out, Hamp immediately left the bar and headed home. Later that night, when taking out the trash, the barkeep found the drunk man lying dead out back in the alley. They arrested Hamp and put him in prison for twelve years for manslaughter," I explained.

As the car rolled to a gentle stop, Hamp got up from my rocking chair and moved closer to Hattie's car. I had never seen Hamp without a big smile on his face, but not today. I could tell by his expression that something was terribly wrong. In a flash, he was beside me, holding my arm as we approached my front porch.

"What's wrong, Hamp?" I asked. "I've never seen you this worked up."

I looked into Hamp's eyes, and they were filled with fright and worry. "Let's sit on the porch, and I'll tell you what's going on," he said.

When we got seated on the porch, I introduced Hattie to Hamp and told him that she was Turkey Holler Bill's daughter.

Hamp said, "I loved your mother, and I'm extremely sorry for your loss. That's one of the reasons I'm here. It's only fitting that I come and pay my respects to Hattie and to you, Dessie. I also wanted to let you both know that I had nothing to do with

Turkey Holler Bill's murder."

"Murder?" I said. "Turkey Holler fell off a cliff or somewhere on the side of the mountain and dragged herself back to her cabin, where she died from internal injuries. She was bruised and all scraped up but wasn't murdered. Who told you she was?"

"Sheriff Bobby Spillman and some fellow from up north somewhere drove up to my shack yesterday afternoon. The sheriff said that a few days back, somebody broke into Turkey Holler's house and beat her to death. I almost cried. I loved Turkey Holler. We were the best of friends. Then the fellow with Sheriff Bobby spoke up and said, 'Look, my name is Jim Clanton, from Independence, Ohio, and I've done a lot of research on you, Mr. Hamp.' I asked him, 'What are you talking about? What kind of research?' Mr. Clanton said, 'I found out that you are a cold-blooded murderer from Detroit, where you killed a man with your bare hands. I also discovered that you spent twelve years in prison before being paroled and moving to your old shack.' 'I did spend twelve years in prison for something I didn't do,' I said. 'I didn't kill that man in Detroit, and I sure as hell didn't kill my close friend Turkey Holler Bill.' 'Look, let me get to the point,' Mr. Clanton said. 'I'm down here to buy up all the land on Brushy Mountain and the surrounding hills, as well as property in Moravian Falls. Hamp, you own fifty-one acres including this old shack, and I aim to buy it or send you to prison for the rest of your life.' Just then, that crooked sheriff Bobby Spillman spoke up and said, 'Look, Hamp, whether you killed Turkey Holler or not, who's the jury going to believe, you or me? Now, Hamp, we can make all this go away. All you have to do is sell Mr. Clanton your place.' "

"Hamp, they can't prove nothing about Turkey Holler's death. Hattie Mae is going to bury her mama tomorrow. Then what are they going to do?" I said.

"Well, Dessie, I'm scared to death. I told him that I had no family, and finding a place would take some time," Hamp said. "Mr. Clanton spoke up and said, 'Look, Hamp, I'm going to pay you four hundred dollars for each acre. That's over twenty thousand dollars. Surely, you can find a place with that kind of money. I'm going to give you two weeks to sell and be gone, or else.' Then that crooked sheriff Bobby Spillman slapped me on the back and said, 'Sell and move on or go to prison. It's that simple, Hamp.' Both men were laughing when they got back into their truck and drove back toward town. I guess I have no choice but to sell. I wouldn't be able to survive in prison."

"We'll figure something out, Hamp. Try not to worry," I said. "They can't just go around and harass folks and scare them to death. We'll call the law on them crooked scoundrels."

"Dessie, they are the law," said Hamp.

Hattie Mae spoke up and said, "Maybe I can help. My best friend's husband just retired from the FBI in Georgia. He'll know what to do and who to call here in North Carolina for help. I'll call him just as soon as I get back to the motel. I'll let Dessie know what he said tomorrow right after Mama's funeral. Dessie, I better be going. I'll come pick you up at noon tomorrow for the funeral. It's just a graveside service and starts at one o'clock."

"No need, Hattie. You have a lot to worry about, and I already told Mr. Mike that Lou and I would ride with him to your mama's service," I said.

"Can I give you a ride somewhere, Hamp?" asked Hattie.

Hamp said, "No thanks, Miss Hattie. I'm going to head back down the mountain to my place and try to figure out what I'm going to do about that sheriff."

"Hamp, you want to stay here tonight and go with me tomorrow to Turkey Holler's funeral?" I asked.

"Dessie, I'm not going to go to the funeral. I'm sure the sheriff will be there, and I don't want to give him the satisfaction of seeing me worried. I'll walk back up here tomorrow afternoon to pay my respects," said Hamp.

Hattie Mae came over to me for a big hug and said, "I'll see you at the service tomorrow, Dessie. It was a pleasure to meet you, Hamp."

I watched as Hattie drove down the mountain and Hamp headed through my backyard and into the woods to his shack. I thought, *Tomorrow is going to be a rough day. There's the funeral, and Lou and Charlie and others will visit. I should eat a quick bite and turn in early.*

"How are you holding up, Miss Mary? Should we stop for a while and let you rest some?" I asked.

"No way, Dessie. I want to finish this story, no matter how long it takes," said Mary.

CHAPTER TEN

"Dessie, wake up and let me in! It's already after seven, and the sun has been up for at least an hour," yelled Lou while banging on my bedroom window.

"I'm up, I'm up! I'll meet you at the front door in just a minute," I yelled back.

While I was putting on my robe, I took a glance at the clock and saw that it was just two minutes past seven. Making my way to the door, I yelled, "Leave them dogs on the front porch, Lou! It's been raining, and I don't want my house to smell like wet hounds."

When I opened the door, Lou was making all her wet dogs lie down, calling each one by name. Lou was dressed in a new pair of overalls with a tan flannel shirt and her wool army coat, along with her Sears rubber boots. Lou's red eyes told me that she had been crying for a long time.

"Lou, for heaven's sake, why are you here so early? The funeral isn't until one, and Mike won't be here until about twelve to pick us up," I said.

Lou walked by me and, once inside, pulled Little Beaver out from under her coat and laid him gently on my sofa. "Little Beaver and I have been up all night crying our eyes out," she said. "Today, I have to bury my sister and Hattie Mae has to bury her mama. I been thinking about it all night, and I don't think I'll be able to live without Turkey Holler Bill."

"Lou, calm down. It's going to be hard, not being able to visit with Turkey Holler, and I'm sure you're going to miss her something terrible. As each day passes, it will get a little easier to live without Ida, but you'll always have the memories of her and you," I said, trying to calm her down.

Little Beaver moved across my sofa, laid his head on Lou's lap, and licked her hand. Lou just kept sobbing as I went into the kitchen to pour us a cup of coffee.

"Can I fix you some fried eggs and grits for breakfast?" I asked Lou while handing her a cup.

"Lord no, Dessie. As tore up as I am about Ida's funeral, if I eat anything, I'll be sick," said Lou.

I went into the kitchen, leaving Lou and Little Beaver crying and sobbing on the sofa. I fixed my breakfast and cleaned up the kitchen and told Lou that I was going into the bedroom to get dressed for the day. I found and ironed my dark blue Sunday dress and decided that it would be appropriate to wear it to Turkey Holler Bill's funeral. After I got dressed, I went back into the living room. When I sat down, I tried my best to calm Lou. I tried to talk about when she and Ida were little and some of the messes they got into. Thinking back, Lou slowed down from crying to tell me some stories about her and Turkey Holler. Then, with no warning, Lou burst out crying even harder.

I thought, *It sure is going to be a rough and long day.* My thoughts were interrupted when I heard a truck approaching on my old dirt road. I went to the front door and saw that Mike had arrived and parked at my mailbox and was making his way to the house. I opened the door and walked onto the porch, waving.

When Mike got on the porch, I said, "Let me warn you, Lou is beside herself and has been crying ever since she got here this morning."

Mike said, "Dessie, I'm sure she'll get to feeling better after the service and after she talks with Charlie."

"Charlie has always been sort of a father figure to Lou, and I'm sure that if anyone can calm her down, Charlie could," I said.

Mike and I went into the house to help Lou put her coat on, and then we got her into the backseat of the truck.

Mike said, "Lou, you and Dessie are more than welcome in my truck, but those dogs have got to stay on the porch."

Lou whimpered, "Little Beaver will look after them while we're burying my sister, but I want to get right back to them once the funeral is over. My babies can't be away from me for more than a few hours or they'll worry themselves to death."

Lou cried all the way down the mountain but slowed after we got to the Baptist church and the gravesites in Moravian Falls. When Mike pulled into the parking lot of the church, I noticed that the rain had stopped and that several people were already mingling at the graveyard. Mike helped Lou and me get out of the truck and walked with us through the entrance of the graveyard. Once inside the gates, I saw a freshly dug grave covered with a big green tent and a few metal folding chairs around the site. There were several folks standing behind the chairs, waiting for the family to be seated.

At the funeral, as expected, were Hattie Mae, Charlie, Dorothy (Charlie's third wife, long divorced), Lou, myself, Mike, Preacher Wright and his wife, Mary, Ken Martin and his wife Shelby, April Brandon (the egg lady), and Michael Langford. Also at the graveside service were my third-oldest son, Bill Pennell, and my next-to-youngest son, Don Pennell. I was not surprised to see Bill and Don there. They loved Turkey Holler Bill. When they were just little boys, Bill and Don used to hike up the mountain to visit Ida, sometimes staying all day until almost dark. When Bill and Don got back home, they would tell me about all the adventures and mischief they and Turkey Holler Bill had gotten into.

I didn't expect and did not appreciate to see Sheriff Bobby

Spillman, Frail Jones, and that mean old Billy Barr. I thought, *These three men were nothing but hateful to Turkey Holler Bill. I guess they want to torture her and her family to death.*

Lou and Hattie Mae cried during the entire service, and especially when they lowered the casket into the grave. Lou cried so much and so hard that she hyperventilated and fainted.

Charlie said, "Bill, help me get Lou into my truck, and I'll take her to Dessie's house. I'll gather up her dogs and then take her to her place. I'll give her a little shine, and she'll be calm as a cucumber and asleep in no time."

Dorothy spoke up and said, "Charlie, you better not drink any of that shine. It's going to kill you if you don't quit drinking that stuff."

Charlie spoke up loudly and announced that he hadn't had a drink in over three months. He said, "My shine is for selling and not drinking. Yep, I'm on the wagon."

Soon, my porch was packed with people that had attended the funeral. Hattie Mae, Preacher Wright and his wife, Dorothy, and myself took up all the rocking chairs. Mike, Bill, and Don got straight-back chairs from the kitchen and brought them into the front yard for folks to sit.

Hattie Mae said, "Dessie, let me help you carry the coffee tray and cups onto the porch, along with your famous oatmeal cookies."

Once we got into the kitchen, Hattie Mae told me that after the service, she was confronted by Billy Barr, and that he caused a big ruckus. Hattie said he claimed that her mama's land was rightly his. "He said that his family was the first to settle on Mama's land. He claimed that my daddy basically stole it from his family, and he wanted it back."

"Hattie, you best stay clear of Billy Barr. I think he's capable of almost anything," I said.

"You're right, Dessie. He got real upset and almost physical when I told him that he could buy it back this Saturday at the auction. I believe he would have hit me if Michael Langford hadn't stepped in and pushed him away. Billy said that was not the last I would see of him. He cussed me and Michael all the way to his truck," said Hattie.

"Hattie, I'm so sorry that happened to you. Some of these mountain folks can get kind of crazy sometimes, especially some of these old codgers that think they can beat you out of something," I said. "Let's get the cookies and coffee onto the porch for our guests. I can hear Dorothy fussing about being hungry, not to mention that I haven't offered her so much as a cup of coffee. We'll talk more when everyone leaves."

CHAPTER ELEVEN

I noticed when Hattie and I got back to the front porch that the sun had come out and all the rain clouds were gone. Most all the guests were quietly talking about what was going on in their lives or telling stories about Turkey Holler Bill and some of her adventures. I saw that Hamp had made his way up the mountain and joined Mike Wall and my sons, Bill and Don, sitting under the old poplar tree.

Some of my friends from town brought food up to the house for Hattie Mae and the guests. Most everyone just made themselves at home and went in and out of my house, fixing something to eat and drink.

I sat in the rocking chair beside Dorothy and handed her a big stack of oatmeal cookies and a cup of coffee.

Dorothy said, "I wonder where Charlie is. He should have been back from Lou's a long time ago."

"I suppose that Charlie is making sure Lou has calmed down and that her dogs are fed. You know how much Lou loves them dogs of hers, especially Little Beaver," I said.

Just then, I heard a truck winding its way up the old mountain road. We all watched as Charlie slowly drove next to my mailbox and came to a quick stop. I could tell something was wrong because Charlie practically fell out of the truck when he opened his door. We all watched as he stumbled and staggered his way up to the poplar tree, where Hamp, Mike, Bill, and Don were sitting. It was evident to everyone that Charlie was drunk.

Still sitting in her rocking chair, Dorothy yelled at Charlie, "I thought you had quit drinking! Well, Charlie, I see that you let us all down again."

Charlie, still standing but swaying, yelled back, "Well, no higher up than we was, we didn't have far to fall!"

Mike, Bill, Don, Hamp, and all the other guests burst out laughing—all but Dorothy, who was pissed. She jumped up from her rocking chair and went into the kitchen. When she came back onto the porch, she had wrapped up three pieces of fried chicken and several oatmeal cookies. She stormed off the porch, got into her car, and yelled back at Charlie, "And you wonder why I divorced you years ago!"

Charlie waved his middle finger to tell her goodbye as she drove past my mailbox and down the mountain road.

Still snickering, Bill stood up, took Charlie by the arm, and said, "Come on, Charlie, let's get you some food and coffee. You got a lot of sobering up to do before I'm going to let you drive home."

Several friends and neighbors came to visit for a while and

to pay their respects to Hattie Mae and myself. Charlie finally sobered up enough by late evening to drive home. He and Bill were the last to say goodbye, leaving just Hattie Mae, Hamp, and myself in my living room.

Hattie Mae said, "Hamp, I was glad to see you today. I have what I think is good news for you concerning your land and that crooked sheriff Bobby Spillman. Last night, I called my friend's husband that retired from the FBI. His name is James Parker, and he was chief investigator for the Bureau office in Helen, Georgia. I explained your situation and how the sheriff threatened you with life in prison unless you sold your land to Jim Clanton. This morning before the funeral, he called me back and told me that he has been in touch with an FBI friend of his who retired in the Brushy Mountains."

"Did he say that I best start packing?" asked Hamp.

Hattie Mae said, "No, Hamp, you're not going anywhere. Turns out that our friendly sheriff has been under investigation by the FBI for quite a long time. Several folks in Wilkes County contacted the Bureau with complaints against the sheriff for extortion and bribery, along with one claim that Sheriff Bobby shot an unarmed man he thought was fooling around with his wife."

A look of relief came across Hamp's face as he smiled and said, "That man must be blind, 'cause I've seen the sheriff's wife. She's a great big woman, and she sure is ugly. The farmers sitting around the grocery store claim she's so ugly that you could mash her face in dough and make gorilla cookies."

Hattie Mae said, "He suggested that you just hold tight, Hamp, until they conclude their investigation. He also suggested that if push comes to shove, you should move in with a family member until this is settled."

"Speaking of moving in, it's getting late, and I have to walk back down the mountain to my place," said Hamp. "Hattie, I can't thank you enough for all you've done for me. You saved my life, and I'll be forever grateful. If there is anything I can ever do for you, all you have to do is ask."

Hamp got up from the sofa, put on his old coat and red hunting cap, hugged me and then Hattie, said good night, and headed out the door and down the mountain.

Hattie said, "Okay, Dessie, I'm not leaving until I help you clean up and wash all those dishes in the sink."

I said, "Hattie, those dishes will still be there in the morning, and I'll take care of them then."

Hattie simply walked into the kitchen, put on an apron, and started on the dishes. She washed them in one sink while I rinsed them in the other. I hadn't realized that just about every dish, pot, pan, glass, and bowl I owned had been used. It took us at least an hour before the task was done.

I convinced Hattie to have one more cup of coffee and a couple cookies while we visited.

Hattie said, "Dessie, thank you for today, for your support, and for inviting all Mama's friends and family into your home. You made a difficult situation easier, and I don't know what I would have done without you. I love you and will for the rest of my life."

I stood up, hugged Hattie, and whispered, "I love you, too, and your sweet mama."

Hattie said, "It's ten-thirty. I need to get back to the motel and try to get some sleep. I need to get as much rest as possible so I can think clearly at the auction this Saturday."

"Hattie, I have a great idea," I said. "I have an extra bedroom, and you're more than welcome to spend the night with me. That way, in the morning, we can have a nice breakfast and head to town to see how many signs Michael Langford has put up regarding the auction. We can even have lunch at the Moravian Café and do a little shopping around town."

Hattie said, "Dessie, I don't want to be a bother to you anymore."

"I would love for you to stay the night," I said.

I took her by the arm, led her into the spare bedroom, and

cut on the overhead light and the lamp on the nightstand. I helped Hattie turn down the comforter, and then I went to the closet and took down a handmade quilt in case she got cold. I then hugged her good night, closed her door, and retired to my bedroom.

Later, I was startled awake by someone knocking loudly on my bedroom door. I got up and opened the door to find Hattie shaking uncontrollably. She whispered, "There's a man in the yard looking in the windows."

I grabbed Hattie's hand. Without turning on the light, we moved to her bedroom window. I looked out and saw just a big, bright full moon, lots of shadows, and poplar leaves blowing across the yard.

I said, "Hattie, I don't see a thing. You must have been dreaming, or maybe a stray dog was in the yard. It's a full moon tonight, and the wind and these old hills can play tricks on you. Do you think you can go back to sleep, or would you like a warm glass of milk to help you drift back off?"

Hattie said, "Dessie, I'm sure I saw a man in your yard. He was trying to look through the windows. He must have run off when he saw me jump out of bed and run out of my room. No way will I be able to sleep unless I know for sure that no one is out there."

I told Hattie to just sit tight and I would get my shotgun and go out to make sure that no one was around the house. I then went to my bedroom, got my 20-gauge out from under my bed, and headed toward the front door.

Hattie said, "You're not going out of this house alone. I'm going with you. Please be careful with that gun, Dessie."

I opened the front door to a bright, moonlit night with a cool breeze blowing and Hattie hot on my heels. I whispered, "Hattie, please back up just a little. If I have to use this shotgun, I need a little room to raise it to my shoulder."

When I started down the steps from my porch, Hattie was so close I thought I might fall. I decided it would be better if she walked beside me, so if I had to use the gun, I would have enough room, and she could see for herself that no one was hiding in my yard.

I held her arm as she moved beside me. We searched every square inch of my front yard and backyard, and not once did Hattie let go of my nightgown.

When we made our way back into the house, I could see signs of relief on Hattie's face.

"I'm so sorry I woke you up, Dessie, but I could have sworn there was a man snooping around, trying to look into the windows," said Hattie.

I said, "It's okay, Hattie. You were sleeping in a strange place, and you had to bury your mama today, not to mention these old hills can be spooky, especially at night. Now, let's get you some warm milk, and maybe you can get a few hours of sleep before it's daylight."

I got up early the next morning and fixed a big pot of coffee. I decided to let Hattie sleep in a while. She had gone through a rough day yesterday and then an almost sleepless night.

It was almost nine before I heard Hattie moving around in her room. Soon, she was dressed and sitting at the kitchen table while I fixed breakfast. I got my old cast-iron skillet greased up and placed it on a hot burner. When I started cooking several pieces of country ham, the kitchen and the whole house smelled delicious. While the ham was cooking, I put a big pan of country biscuits in the oven and fried several eggs in another pan. After I cooked the ham, I used the same pan and the ham grease and made redeye gravy. I served Hattie the eggs and ham on a big kitchen plate and poured the redeye gravy in a separate bowl surrounded by biscuits.

"Believe it or not, Dessie, this is the first time I have ever eaten redeye gravy," Hattie said as she placed her biscuit into the gravy bowl. "It is absolutely delicious. What's in it, and how do you make it?"

"It's simple to make, Hattie. You just take your cast-iron skillet and add a little oil while frying your favorite country ham. Once the ham is done, I add a blend of black coffee and water to the hot pan and ham drippings. I take a big wooden spoon and stir, making sure I scrape all the ham pieces from the bottom of the pan. I bring the gravy to a full boil and cook it for about five minutes. It's that simple," I said as I poured us another cup of coffee.

"Dessie, maybe you can teach me how to make redeye gravy and these great biscuits," Hattie said.

I said, "Hattie, it would be my pleasure."

It didn't take us long to clean up the kitchen and get dressed for our trip into town. Hattie held on to my arm as we made our way through the front yard toward her car, parked by the mailbox. I was looking down to make sure I didn't stumble when I saw a cigarette butt lying in a small pile of leaves. I immediately thought about Hattie claiming that a man was in the yard, trying to look into the windows. I thought, *Maybe Hattie was right. Maybe there was someone last night trying to see who was in the house.* Then I remembered all the folks that came by yesterday to pay their respects, and I thought, *I didn't see anyone smoking, but there were so many folks coming and going. I'm sure one of them probably dropped a cigarette butt without even thinking about it.* I wanted to spend a pleasant day with Hattie, and I sure didn't want her to worry over a simple cigarette, so I never mentioned it to her.

Soon, we were driving past the Noah Hole and Mike's house as we made our way down the mountain. When we got to town, I noticed that they had put up a new sign that said, "Welcome to Moravian Falls." We drove to the town square and parked in front of City Florist.

Hattie said, "Dessie, let's go shopping in the florist shop.

I want to buy you a plant for all you've done for me and my mama."

I told Hattie that it was a pleasure to look after her and her mama, and that there was no need for her to spend money on me. Hattie, however, was having none of it and insisted on going plant shopping. It wasn't long until she bought a beautiful red azalea and placed it on the backseat floorboard of her car.

Next, we started walking around the square, doing a lot of window shopping and counting all the signs that Michael Langford had put up about the auction this Saturday.

Hattie said, "If the number of signs is any indication, then this auction will be a big success."

I told Hattie that I hoped it would be as well, but not to get her hopes up too high. I told her that nobody on our mountain had much money or even had a steady job. Most all the folks on the mountain made a living off the land in the apple orchards, selling garden vegetables, or digging and selling ginseng roots. In fact, the only person I knew that had a steady job was Frail Jones. The government paid rent for the use of his land where they built the fire tower. They also paid him to keep a watch out for forest fires. People who had been up in the tower said you could see everybody's house that lived on the mountain and their coming and goings.

"I won't, Dessie. I just want it to be all over. Michael

Langford said the most likely buyer would be someone from a surrounding county," said Hattie.

"It's after twelve. Would you like to get a bite of lunch?" I said, trying to change the subject. "The Moravian Café has great burgers and French fries and the best apple pie you've ever eaten."

Hattie and I both ate cheeseburgers and fries—and yes, we had a piece of that apple pie. After lunch, we continued shopping around our little town. At each shop where we stopped, I would introduce Hattie to my friends who owned the stores. They all told Hattie how sorry they were to hear the news about Turkey Holler Bill and offered their condolences. Some folks asked about her mama's place and the upcoming auction. Some of the nosiest people asked Hattie how much she hoped to sell the place for. Hattie just smiled. I thought, *How rude and inconsiderate some folks can be.*

When it started to get close to two in the afternoon, I asked Hattie if she was ready to go back up the mountain, as it was getting late and I needed to put some pintos on for supper.

"Dessie, I have a great idea," said Hattie. "While we were in the Moravian Café, I saw that they have fried chicken and all the fixings on the menu. How about we stop by and get our supper and then head on up the mountain? If you don't mind, Dessie, I would like to spend another night with you, if that's okay with you."

"I would love for you to stay with me as long as you like," I said.

Much to my surprise and delight, Hattie said, "After we get our supper from the café, I'll stop by the motel and gather some of my things. I might even stay with you until after the auction this Saturday. I love you, Dessie, and I want to spend as much time as I can with you." She had a big smile on her face.

We got our supper from the café and drove up the old mountain road. When we passed by Mike Wall's house, I noticed that Mike's truck was not in his driveway. I thought, *Mike must be visiting with friends, or maybe he went into town to run some errands. He is such a great friend and neighbor, and I don't know what I would do without him.*

When we got to the top of the mountain and rounded the last curve leading to my place, Hattie shouted, "What is that sorry sheriff Bobbie Spillman doing at your mailbox with all his blue lights flashing, and who is that sitting in the back of his squad car?"

CHAPTER THIRTEEN

W e stopped directly behind his squad car, and as I got out, I could plainly see that Sheriff Bobby Spillman had Charlie in the backseat. The first thought I had was that the sheriff had arrested Charlie for driving drunk. But if so, why would they be at my house?

The sheriff opened the backseat door, and I saw that Charlie was extremely upset and crying. He got out of the car, grabbed me by the hand, and said, "Dessie, let's go to the porch and sit. Something terrible has happened."

"Tell me right here, right now, Charlie. What's wrong?" I asked.

"Lou is dead!" cried Charlie.

My knees buckled, and I would have fallen except for Charlie's tight grip on my hand. I immediately became sick on my stomach as a flow of tears rolled down my face. Charlie still held my hand, and Hattie Mae was behind me. Together, they led me to my rocking chair.

After a moment, I cried out, "My poor Lou! How? Why? What happened?"

"I drove up to Lou's place just a little after noon," said

Charlie. "I parked down by her mailbox and made my way up to the house. When I got close to the front porch, I found Lou lying face up in a pool of blood. She had a huge wound in the middle of her chest, and her blood was still soaking through her clothes and onto the ground. Beside her and touching her hand was her old 410 shotgun. Also scattered around were several empty shotgun shells, and the yard was full of dead dogs."

"Charlie drove to town and got me, and together we drove up to Lou's place," said Sheriff Bobby Spillman. "It appears to me that Lou shot all her dogs and then turned the gun on herself. After seeing Lou at Turkey Holler Bill's funeral, I figure she was so distraught that she took her own life."

"No, sheriff, you're wrong. Someone killed Lou," I said. "Even if she was so tore up as to kill herself, she would never shoot her dogs. They were the same as her children. Someone killed my cousin, and I wouldn't put it past you to have done it, Sheriff Bobby Spillman."

The sheriff turned his back to me. As he walked to his squad car, he turned his head and said, "Dessie, I know you're in shock, so I'm going to try to forget you said that. The medical examiner is up at Lou's place right now, and he will determine if it was suicide or if there's a cold-blooded killer on this mountain."

I could almost detect a slight smile on the sheriff's face as he got into his car and headed back down the mountain with his blue lights still flashing.

I said to Charlie and Hattie, "Hell, the medical examiner is Bobby Spillman's brother, and he's as crooked as Bobby. Hattie, will you drive Charlie to the sheriff's office so he can get his truck and then follow him back up here to get me? The three of us are going over to Lou's place. I want to see what happened myself."

Hattie said, "Dessie, I'm afraid to leave you alone."

I told Hattie and Charlie to go on and get the truck, that I would be all right. I told them I felt sick on my stomach and needed some time to get over the shock of my poor old Lou's death.

While Hattie and Charlie were gone, I thought, *There's no way that Lou took her own life. Even if she decided to kill herself, she would not under any circumstances shoot her dogs. Lou loved those old mutt dogs and looked after them the same as you would a child, especially Little Beaver.*

I began to think, *Who would want poor old Lou dead? That sorry sheriff is the first person to come to mind. Lou ran Sheriff Bobby Spillman and that fellow from Ohio off her land with her 410 shotgun. The sheriff and Jim Clanton might have revisited with Lou about selling her place, and things got out of hand, and they killed Lou. Heck, they threatened old Hamp with prison, so I wouldn't put murder past them.*

I thought, *It could have been that mean old Billy Barr that killed Lou. He always claims the whole mountain belongs to him. He's always running on with some story that he and his family owned it all and were somehow beat out of their land. Rumor on the mountain has it that Billy Barr killed his first wife with poison and froze the second one to death. He and Hattie had words after her mama's service, and Michael Langford had to step in to save her.*

Then I thought, *It could have been a total stranger from town. Folks have been gossiping, and Lou may have bragged about how she paid cash for Turkey Holler Bill's funeral. Someone may have paid Lou a visit looking for money and just decided to kill her.*

At least I knew that Lou would not have killed herself. Someone on this mountain or in town was a cold-blooded killer.

My thoughts were interrupted when I heard the familiar sound of Charlie's truck getting closer to my house. Hattie Mae and Charlie came to the porch and helped me to the truck. Tears were still running down Charlie's cheeks.

It was about four o'clock when we got to Lou's place. There were cars and trucks parked everywhere. Some had flashing lights, while others looked like they might belong to the Forest Service or the game wardens. The entire front yard and house were surrounded by yellow tape, and there were red flags stuck in the ground.

Sheriff Bobby motioned us to stop as he walked up to the truck. Charlie rolled down his window, and Sheriff Bobby said, "Y'all don't need to be here. You should turn that truck around and head home. I still have an active investigation going on, and I don't want y'all to mess it up."

"Listen here, that's my cousin that has been killed, and I aim to look at Lou myself," I said.

Sheriff Bobby said, "Well, Dessie, if you want to look at Lou's body, you'll have to visit her at the funeral parlor. We have already ruled her death a suicide, and I had her body removed about thirty minutes ago. Y'all can come back tomorrow after we get everything cleaned up and see for yourself."

I burst out in tears and was reaching for the door handle when Charlie said, "Now, Dessie, we don't want to start no kind of ruckus. We'll come back first thing in the morning. Besides, Lou is gone, and there is nothing we can do or say that will bring her back."

I cried all the way back home and kept thinking, *I wonder what that sorry sheriff Bobby Spillman meant when he said they needed to get everything cleaned up.*

CHAPTER FOURTEEN

I drifted in and out of sleep that night. I just couldn't get Lou's murder off my mind. Hattie slept in the spare bedroom and Charlie on the sofa in the living room.

I apparently drifted off and was startled when Hattie tapped on my bedroom door and said, "Dessie, it's morning. I've fixed you and Charlie a light breakfast."

I got dressed and went into the kitchen to see Charlie and Hattie had already fixed a cup of coffee and eaten a scrambled egg sandwich. Hattie poured me a cup of coffee and prepared me a plate of scrambled eggs and toast. I thanked her but told her I was still way too upset to even think about eating. I told Charlie to get my shotgun out from under my bed and put it in his old truck. I was thinking I had better carry a gun to Lou's house, since God only knew what or who we might encounter.

Soon, we were headed up the old mountain road to Lou's shack. I knew that I had to go see for myself what happened to poor old Lou, but believe me, I dreaded every minute of the ride. Charlie parked his truck at Lou's run-down mailbox. The first thing I noticed was the yellow sheriff's tape surrounding the entire front yard and extending around the side of the house and all the way to Lou's shed.

The three of us began to make our way up the path toward Lou's front porch. The sight of bloody dead dogs lying throughout the front yard was sickening. As we got closer to the house, I saw a huge pool of dried blood where my poor Lou's body had lain. I couldn't hold back the tears, and my knees got weak. Hattie held my arm and tried to comfort me.

"I thought Sheriff Bobby said they were going to clean up. Looks like to me the only cleaning they did was to see what they could steal from Lou's house," said Charlie.

It was evident that someone had ransacked the house. The front door was wide open, and I saw a lot of Lou's things thrown onto the porch. When we got to the steps, I told Charlie to go to the shed and get a shovel and bury all of Lou's dogs.

"I'll dig a big hole in that old apple orchard across the road from Lou's mailbox and bury them all together," said Charlie.

I told Charlie that would not be proper. I told him they were her children, and that each one should have a proper grave with some kind of marker. Charlie just shrugged his shoulders and headed toward Lou's shed.

Hattie helped me up the steps, and we both walked into the main room of Lou's house. There in the middle of the floor was Lou's straw bed, which was cut and torn. I told Hattie that someone must have figured that Lou hid her money in that old mattress. The fireplace was full of ashes and a couple of burnt logs that were still warm. The dresser that held Lou's long underwear and her flannel shirts was turned on its side. All the drawers were emptied and the clothes thrown around on the floor. When we got to the closet, it was evident that it had also been ransacked. All of Lou's coats were lying on the floor in a pile. Each one of the coat pockets was turned inside out. Lou had a shoebox she kept on the closet shelf that held all her letters, cards, bills, and pictures. The shoebox had been emptied and dumped on the floor beside her coats. I picked up all the letters, cards, and pictures and placed them back into the shoebox.

Hattie took out one piece of paper at a time and carefully unfolded each of them. There was an old Christmas card from Lou's husband that was mailed from Fort Ord, California. The face of the card had a picture of a big Santa all dressed in glitter and red. She opened the card slowly, and out fell a piece of Teaberry and a piece of Clove chewing gum. Hattie read the card: "Love you and miss you. Merry Christmas. Your husband, Hank."

I thought, *What a dummy!* Who else would Lou have thought Hank was? Charlie used to say that the army was the perfect place for Hank because as dumb as he was, he couldn't make it in the real world, even on Brushy Mountain.

In the letters and cards, Hattie found a brown grocery bag that had been carefully folded. On the outside, someone had written in big, bold letters, **LOU ADAMS, LAST WILL AND TESTAMENT.**

Hattie carefully opened the grocery bag and read, "If anything should ever happen to me, and I die, I want everything I own give to my uncle Charlie. Charlie always checked on me. He made sure I had something to eat, firewood, and a coat. Every week, he always brought me a quart jar of shine. If Charlie leaves this world before me, then I leave all I own and have to my sweet aunt Dessie Pennell. I also want Dessie to have all my dogs, because she loves them as much as I do."

At the bottom was Lou's name in big, bold letters: **SIGNED, LOU ADAMS.**

My tears began to flow again as I thought about Lou and her dogs that she loved so much, and how Lou loved Charlie and me and had made a will leaving it all to Charlie, even if it was written on a paper grocery bag.

Hattie found several pictures of men in their Confederate uniforms proudly holding on to their old muskets. I guess these were pictures of her grandpa and other relatives that fought in the Civil War. The last picture Hattie found was one of Turkey Holler Bill, her mama. Turkey Holler was dressed in overalls with a flannel shirt and was leaning on the old hickory tree close to her shack. She held her shotgun and was proudly displaying six squirrels that she had shot.

"May I have this picture of Mama?" asked Hattie.

I just smiled and said, "Sure you can, honey."

Hattie and I were shocked when we entered Lou's kitchen. Someone had removed all the knives, silverware, and plates and neatly placed them on the kitchen table. It almost looked like someone was preparing the table for dinner. All of the old cast-iron pots and pans were also removed from the cabinets and placed on the kitchen floor. I thought, *I wonder who would destroy the house but then take the time to neatly place the silverware and plates, as well as the pots and pans.*

We had been at the house for about two hours when Charlie yelled from the front yard for Hattie and me to come see where he buried Lou's dogs. When we walked onto the front porch, we saw Charlie leaning on a shovel and standing at the mailbox. When we got to the mailbox, Charlie took me by the arm and led us into the apple orchard toward a flat, grassy area.

"Look, Dessie, I gave each one of them dogs a proper burial. I even placed a big mountain rock on top of every grave," Charlie said.

I walked by the dogs' graves and thought of Lou and how much she loved her babies. When I got to the last one, I had counted only ten graves.

"Charlie, Lou had eleven dogs, but there are only ten graves," I said.

"I couldn't find Little Beaver. He must have run off and hid when all the shooting started," Charlie said.

I told Charlie that he was probably right, or that Little Beaver had been wounded and ran off and died somewhere else.

While we headed back to the house, I stopped every few steps and hollered for Little Beaver to come. But there was no sign of Lou's favorite dog.

When we got back into the house, Charlie and I picked up the dresser chest and began to put back its drawers. That's when we heard Hattie scream from the kitchen.

I then heard a man yell, "What the hell are you screaming for?"

CHAPTER FIFTEEN

When I got to the kitchen, there was a rough-looking man sitting at the table. He looked like he was waiting on his lunch to be served.

"Frail Jones, what in the world are you doing here?" I demanded.

"I was in the fire tower when I saw Charlie's old truck coming up the mountain. I figured y'all was up here to get Lou's stuff. I sure was sorry to hear the news that Lou killed herself. I saw from the tower all the police cars here yesterday and decided to drive down and see what was going on. Sheriff Bobby told me that Lou killed herself, and then he made me leave," said Frail.

"Well, you scared the devil out of Hattie and me," I said.

"While y'all were down in the orchard, I just came in and made myself at home," said Frail.

"Frail Jones, I know you didn't come down here just to visit. What's on your mind?" said Charlie.

"I was talking to Lou for the last month or so about selling me this place. Now that Lou is dead, I figure she left this shack and land to you or Dessie, and I thought I would come visit and talk to y'all about selling it to me," said Frail.

That's when I lost it and told Frail that Lou's body wasn't even cold yet, and he had a lot of nerve to come down here to talk about buying her home. I told him to get the hell off Lou's property and not to come back.

Frail smiled as he stood up from the kitchen table and said, "Now, Dessie, don't get your bloomers in such a wad. I'm going to buy Turkey Holler Bill's land at the auction tomorrow, and then I'll buy Lou's place from y'all one way or another."

Charlie walked Frail out of the house and into the front yard and demanded for him to get the hell out of there and not come back.

After the three of us calmed down, Hattie suggested that we walk around Lou's property to see if we could find Little Beaver. We searched all around Lou's shack, down by the creek, and even around her old shed, all the while calling Little Beaver's name. There was no sign of him, and we guessed that he had been wounded and ran off somewhere and died.

Around noon, we decided that we should go back to my house and get ready for the auction tomorrow. Michael Langford planned to stop by and talk to Hattie to let her know what to expect.

Hattie gathered up the shoebox filled with Lou's letters and cards, and the three of us got in Charlie's truck for the short trip home. When we drove around the last curve to my house, I saw that Mike Wall was parked at my mailbox. In the passenger side of Mike's truck sat his friend Michael Langford. Mike and Michael usually ate breakfast together every morning at the Moravian Café.

When Charlie stopped the truck, Mike Wall was quick to my side to help me walk to my front porch and settle into my rocking chair.

"Mike Wall, you're such a polite and sweet young man," I said.

"I promised my good friend Jack that I would look after you, and that's exactly what I aim to do. Plus, I love you as much as I did my grandma," explained Mike. "While Michael and I were eating breakfast at the café this morning, it was all abuzz about what happened to Lou. I was worried about you and Hattie and decided to come up to visit and see if there is anything I can do for y'all."

I told Mike and Mr. Langford what happened that morning over at Lou's place with that good-for-nothing Frail Jones. I also told them Charlie had run Frail off the property and told him never to come back.

Charlie interrupted and said, "Dessie, I can't stay. I've got to get down to the river and check on my place. I need to make sure that some old jackleg hasn't made off with my moonshine still."

I told Charlie to put my shotgun on my bed before he left, and that I would see him around noon tomorrow.

When Charlie's truck was heading down the mountain, Hattie said, "Dessie, I know what's on your mind. I'll put the coffee on and get that pitcher of iced tea out of the refrigerator."

While Hattie was in the kitchen, my new telephone rang. At first, I didn't know what the sound was or where it was coming from. I had owned my phone for only a few days and wasn't used to it ringing.

Hattie yelled from the kitchen, "Dessie, your phone is ringing! I'll get it if you like."

I heard Hattie pick up the phone and say, "Hello. Yes, Mr. Buford, Dessie is here, but she has visitors. If you'll give me your number, I'll make sure she calls you back as quickly as possible."

A short time later, Hattie came back onto the porch with iced tea and coffee and told me that Mr. Buford from down at the funeral parlor wanted me to call him back as soon as I could.

"I wonder how old man Buford got my telephone number," I said to Hattie.

Mike Wall spoke up and said, "Dessie, I saw Mr. Buford at

the café this morning, and we were talking about your cousins Lou and Turkey Holler Bill. Buford said that he needed to talk to you. I gave him your telephone number. I hope you don't mind."

I told Mike that I didn't mind at all. I figured Buford wanted to make Lou's funeral arrangements, but most of all, I figured he wanted to know if he would get paid by me or by the state.

After Hattie poured Mr. Langford a big glass of iced tea, she sat down in the rocker beside him and asked, "What should I expect at the auction tomorrow, Mr. Langford?"

"Remember, my name is Michael, and not Mr. Langford," he said. "I have ten potential cash buyers that have committed to be at the auction tomorrow. There will be three from Forsyth County, three from Yadkin County, and four from here in Wilkes County. I expect there will be a couple folks from town and maybe a couple from this old mountain, but I do not consider them to be potential buyers."

"Why would they not be potential buyers?" Hattie asked.

"Remember when we met at my office, we discussed that the auction would be one sale and one cash buyer, and gross proceeds should be somewhere around $600 per acre. That's $48,900, and quite frankly, most folks from Moravian and those that live on the mountain can't afford a cash payment of that amount," explained Michael.

Michael said that his ten potential buyers would meet at his office the next day at two in the afternoon and ride together up to the auction. Mike Wall had agreed to help drive Michael's customers to Turkey Holler Bill's place.

I told Michael that Charlie would bring Hattie and myself to Turkey Holler Bill's for the auction, and that we would arrive about one-thirty.

Mike Wall stood up, handed Hattie his empty tea glass, and said, "We will see you ladies tomorrow. Remember, Dessie, if you need anything, I'm just a phone call away."

While Mike and Michael headed for the truck, my phone rang from the living room. Hattie got up from her rocking chair and answered it. She said, "Hello, Mr. Buford. Yes, I'll tell Dessie right away." She turned to me. "Mr. Buford said he's on his way up here right now."

"Mary, do you need to take a break?" I asked.

Mary refused to stop even for a cup of hot coffee. I told her that I would get us both another cup and a couple cookies. "If I'm going to be up all night reliving these tragedies, I need all the strength I can muster, not to mention I don't want my blood sugar to drop," I said.

Mary looked very comfortable as she opened a new notebook and retrieved a fresh ink pen. "Whenever you're ready, Miss Dessie, so am I," she said.

CHAPTER SIXTEEN

I thought, *What is so urgent that old man Buford would drive up this mountain to visit with me, especially on a Friday evening?*

My thoughts were interrupted when Hattie said, "Dessie, I put a pound of frozen hamburger in the refrigerator this morning, thinking I would make us hamburger steak with cheddar cheese for our supper. I'll fry some potatoes and onions and make some cornbread to go with the hamburger steak. I'll also open a can of green beans from your garden, if you'd like."

I told Hattie that would be great, and that I was sure getting used to her being around here, and that I didn't ever want her to leave.

Hattie just smiled and said, "I'll be here until I get paid for the sale of Mama's place, and after that, I'll be back to visit as much as possible."

Just then, I heard the all-too-familiar sound of a car approaching my old mountain home. I went to the front door and saw a long black hearse parked down by my mailbox.

I couldn't help smiling at the sight of the hearse. All my mountain neighbors would be gossiping, *Poor old Dessie. First Turkey Holler Bill, then Lou, and now Dessie.*

But not me, not yet. I'm healthy and right as the mail, I thought.

I watched as old man Buford struggled getting out of his hearse and made his way to the front door. When I opened it, I noticed a strange, almost scared look on his face.

Before he even sat down, he said, "Dessie, we need to talk. Something terrible is wrong."

Hattie then came into the living room and greeted Buford. When she saw the look on his face, she asked me if everything was okay. I assured her that I was fine and asked if she would be so kind as to bring Buford a cup of coffee.

Hattie went back to the kitchen to get the coffee, and Buford said, "Dessie, what I have to tell you needs to be just between you and me. I prefer that Hattie not know anything about it."

I told Buford that anything he had to say to me, he could say in front of Hattie. I trusted her as if she were my own daughter.

Hattie brought a tray of coffee and cookies from the kitchen and set it on the table by the sofa.

Old man Buford, still standing but trembling, said, "Lou did not kill herself. She was murdered! When the medical examiner brought me Lou's body, he said that Lou shot all her dogs and then killed herself. After he left, it didn't take me but a second to determine that there was no way Lou committed suicide. If Lou had shot herself, there would have been gunpowder residue on her old army coat and her clothes."

I fought back tears and told Buford that I had argued with that sorry Bobby Spillman that Lou did not commit suicide. I explained to Buford that, first off, Lou would never shoot her dogs. She loved those dogs like her children. Second, Lou's arms were way too short for her to put the shotgun to her chest and still be able to pull the trigger. Third, Charlie said that when he found Lou, there was a huge gunshot wound in her chest. If she had put the gun to her chest and pulled the trigger, there would have been a small hole in her chest and a large exit hole in her back.

Buford said, "While I was still looking over Lou's body, the sheriff pulled his squad car up to the front door of the funeral parlor. Sheriff Bobby and some other feller came into the back of the parlor, where I had Lou. Sheriff Bobby demanded to know if there was anyone else in the building. When I assured him that there wasn't, the other guy spoke up and said his name was Jim Clanton from Independence, Ohio. I asked the sheriff if I could speak to him alone about how Lou died. That's when the sheriff's expression changed and he told me to mind my own business. that it was suicide, plain and simple. Then Jim Clanton spoke up and said, 'Look, Buford, I'm here in Moravian Falls to buy up all the land on Brushy Mountain, as well as some of the businesses and property in town.' Jim Clanton said he was going to develop all of the mountain to build an amusement park and turn Moravian into a quaint village with retail shops, fancy hotels, and restaurants. Jim Clanton said that it really didn't matter how Lou died, the fact was she was dead, and nothing was going to change that. He went on to say that he and Sheriff Bobby figured Lou probably left her property to Dessie, Charlie, or maybe Hattie Mae. Jim Clanton said he wanted me to help him buy Lou's property from the family before it was sold to someone else or, worse, sold at auction. Sheriff Bobby spoke up and told me that he knew your late husband, Hob, and I were friends. He said he figured that I might be able to convince you to sell Lou's place to Mr. Clanton."

Buford told the sheriff that he didn't feel right about claiming Lou killed herself, and he saw no reason to try to convince us to sell Lou's property to Jim Clanton. That was when Sheriff Bobby Spillman got real irate and told him that if he didn't do what they wanted, they would pin Lou's murder on him. He said the sheriff laughed and said, "Buford, I'm the law, and I can make things really bad for you."

Buford said that's when Jim Clanton walked over and put his arm around his shoulders and said that if he helped him buy Lou's property, he would give him ten percent of the sale in cash. He then laughed and told Buford the choice was his, cash or murder.

I told Buford that the sheriff and Mr. Clanton had visited Hamp and basically demanded that Hamp sell his land to Mr.

Clanton or go to prison for killing Turkey Holler Bill.

Buford said that they were not going to pin Lou's murder on him. He took pictures of Lou's body and recorded his findings on a tape recorder. He brought the pictures and the recording to his home and locked them in his safe. He said that he was now suspicious about Turkey Holler's death. He said, "I bought the sheriff's story that Ida probably fell off a cliff or even out of a tree stand while deer hunting." Buford said the sheriff claimed that after the fall, she dragged herself back to her house and died from internal injuries. Buford added, "I don't know about Turkey Holler Bill, but I do know that Lou was murdered, and Dessie, you and Hattie better be careful, especially if it has anything to do with those two." Buford said he was not scared of the sheriff or Mr. Clanton. He said he had friends in the governor's office in Raleigh if they continued to threaten him.

As he was leaving, Buford said that he would see us at the auction tomorrow at Turkey Holler Bill's place, and for us to be safe. He told me he would give Lou a burial just like her sister Ida's, and that I could pay him a little along the way. He said he knew that Charlie and I would pay over time, and that I should not worry about the expense.

When Buford left, I looked over to see Hattie with tears in her eyes. She whispered to me, "Dessie, you reckon somebody killed my poor old mama?"

CHAPTER SEVENTEEN

H attie got up early the next morning and made blueberry pancakes and bacon for breakfast. She said blueberry pancakes were her favorite, and she just knew that she and I were so much alike that they were probably one of my favorites as well.

After breakfast, we sat at the kitchen table drinking coffee and talking about her mama and what Buford had told us the night before. Hattie asked, "If my mama was murdered, how will we be able to find out who killed her, especially if that crooked sheriff is involved?" Hattie said that after the auction, she thought she might call her friend James Parker from the Georgia FBI office and ask for his advice.

While we were still talking about Turkey Holler Bill, I heard Charlie's old truck making its way up the mountain road. As I got up from the table to let him in, I noticed that it was already eleven o'clock, and neither Hattie nor I was dressed for the auction.

When Charlie walked into the house, he said, "If y'all are going to the sale, you best be getting ready. You told Michael Langford you would be there around one-thirty, and I want to leave early enough to find a place to park. Y'all know how narrow Turkey Holler Bill's road is."

After I got dressed, I poured Charlie a cup of coffee and told him about our visit with Buford the night before, and what Buford had said about the sheriff and Jim Clanton.

Charlie's expression changed. He looked as if all the blood in his face was gone. After thinking for what seemed like an hour, Charlie finally spoke up and said, "Well, Dessie, if Turkey Holler Bill was murdered, and we both know that Lou was murdered, then it seems to me that someone is targeting our family. I think that after the auction today, we should just keep quiet and try to forget all that's happened. Let's try to let everything settle down, and maybe that way we can all get back to normal. If we start a ruckus with Bobby Spillman, we could very easily be next on someone's list to kill. He is the law here in Wilkes County, and what he says goes. Why, I even think that old judge down at the courthouse would not cross Sheriff Bobby."

Just then, Hattie Mae came out of her bedroom dressed like she was going to church. She said hello to Charlie and told us she was ready to go to the auction of her mama's place.

Charlie said, "Hattie, I'm not one to tell you what to do, but you might want to wear jeans instead of a dress. You know how rough it is around your mama's place, and besides, if you look like you're well off, your land may not bring as much money."

Hattie said, "What do you mean by well off?"

"Trust me, it's best for you to look like you need every penny you can get from the sale of your mama's place. You don't want people around here to think you don't need the money," Charlie explained.

Hattie said, "Well, in that case, I'll put on some jeans and a ragged old shirt, 'cause Lord knows I do need the money. A retired schoolteacher's pension from the state of Georgia by no means is making anyone well off."

Hattie changed clothes as Charlie suggested, and soon we were in Charlie's truck headed over to Ida's home for the auction. We got there right at one o'clock, and Charlie backed his old truck in between two trees in the front yard. We were the first to arrive, and I asked Hattie, since no one was around, if she would like to go into the house one more time. Hattie started to cry and said no. She said she just wanted everything to be over with so she could try to put her life back together.

The next person to arrive was Frail Jones. He said he saw Charlie's truck from the fire tower and figured that the auction would be starting soon. Frail then approached Hattie and said, "Why don't you just sell this place to me before anyone gets here? That would sure make things a lot easier on you, Hattie."

Hattie asked Frail how he thought selling to him instead of auctioning her mama's place would be easier for her.

Frail said, "Well, maybe not easier, but at least fairer." Frail's voice got louder as he claimed to Hattie that the land really belonged to him anyway, that Hattie's daddy had cheated his daddy out of it during a drunken poker game at Charlie's still.

Charlie got in between Hattie and Frail and sternly said that no one cheated his daddy out of anything. "It was your daddy that decided to drink that shine, and it was also your daddy that wanted to play poker. So just shut up about it, Frail, because at the end of this day, you will have a new neighbor. Maybe you can convince them to sell it to you," said Charlie.

Just then, as Charlie and Frail were arguing, I saw two trucks pull up to the front of Turkey Holler's home and stop down at the mailbox. Michael Langford got out of the first truck and opened the back door for his passengers. Mike Wall parked behind Michael's truck, and five potential buyers got out and stood talking by the mailbox.

Soon, there were more cars and trucks coming up the narrow mountain road. I was not surprised to see Sheriff Bobby Spillman and Jim Clanton park down the road a bit and walk to where a small crowd had gathered. Also parked and walking up the road to Ida's place was my neighbor Preacher Wright, and with him was another neighbor, Mr. Martin. Buford from the funeral parlor was walking behind Mr. Martin. I recognized three or four people from Moravian Falls, and there were some folks from Wilkesboro that I knew.

Charlie said, "Look. There stands old Billy Barr. I wonder what he thinks he's going to buy."

I was shocked when I saw Billy Barr and told Hattie to stay far away from him. I said, "That man is capable of doing anything, and he would not make any bones about it. He is the devil, and Brushy Mountain would be a lot nicer place to live if he wasn't around."

Mike Wall came to the front porch to sit with Charlie, Hattie, and myself while we waited on the auction to begin. Mike said that he counted twenty-three people there, and they all looked like they wanted to buy something. That was sweet of Mike to say, as it made Hattie relax. She even smiled at Mike.

I looked at my watch, and the time was 1:25 P.M. when Michael Langford hooked up a microphone to his truck. He summoned all bidders to gather in the front yard as he stood by his truck at Ida's mailbox. As he was facing all the bidders, Michael handed out plot maps showing the property lines, the house, and the shed.

Michael said, "Ladies and gentlemen, as you know, we are here auctioning Ida Brock's land, consisting of eighty-one and a half acres, house, shed, and everything in them. At the end of the sale, we will have one cash buyer. The buyer must pay within forty-eight hours by certified check or by wire transfer."

Michael said, "If there are no objections, we'll start off the bidding at $600 per acre, for a total of $48,900 for the complete purchase of all of Ida's property. Okay, who's going to start this off with a first bid of $600?"

The crowd was deathly quiet, and although it was only seconds, I could tell that Hattie was extremely nervous.

Seeing that no one in the crowd was going to make the first bid that he asked for, Michael said, "Okay, we'll do it the hard way. Who will give us an opening bid no matter the amount?"

He barely got that question out of his mouth when Billy Barr yelled from the back of the crowd, "I'll give $100 cash money per acre."

Quickly after Michael acknowledged Billy Barr's bid, Frail Jones moved beside where Billy was standing and yelled a bid of $125 per acre.

That's when I noticed that Sheriff Bobby Spillman and Jim Clanton had moved and were standing just behind Billy and Frail.

I was shocked when my neighbor Mr. Martin spoke up and said that he would pay $150 per acre. I suppose he wanted to clear all of Ida's land and plant another apple orchard.

Again, the crowd of bidders was deathly quiet after Michael announced that the high bid was $150 per acre by Mr. Martin.

I looked at Hattie's worried face and smiled to tell her that everything was going to be okay. I whispered to Hattie that this was not Michael Langford's first rodeo, and that he knew exactly what he was doing.

I watched as Michael paced in front of the bidders and announced, "Okay, folks, we have a high bid of $150 per acre. Who will give me $200?"

One of the gentlemen that rode to Ida's place with Mike Wall yelled out, "I'll bid $200 per acre!"

Just as Michael was acknowledging the high bid of $200, Jim Clanton yelled out $250 per acre, cash. Billy Barr and Frail jumped into the fray, both of them bidding at the same time at $275 per acre. Then, arms waving, Billy yelled, "Shut the hell up, Frail! I'm going to buy this place." He quickly bid $300 per acre.

This back-and-forth bidding continued in $25 increments between Frail Jones, Billy Barr, Jim Clanton, and one of Michael's usual bidders. In just a few minutes, I could see looks of tension, almost hatred, on the faces of Billy, Frail, and Mr. Clanton as the high bid reached $725 per acre.

Just then, Jim Clanton announced to the crowd that he was getting tired of those two rednecks, and that his final bid was $850 per acre, totaling $69,275.

The crowd became quiet again, and I saw the anger on Billy Barr's face as he lunged toward Jim Clanton. With one right-hand blow, Billy knocked Mr. Clanton to the ground and said, "I'll show you how a redneck can whip a Yankee's ass!"

As Jim Clanton hit the ground, Sheriff Bobby Spillman pulled his revolver from its holster, aimed it directly at Billy Barr's head, and announced, "Billy, I'll kill you deader than four o'clock if you so much as move a muscle."

CHAPTER EIGHTEEN

B illy was staring at the wrong end of a gun as the sheriff handcuffed him and set him in the backseat of his truck. As Sheriff Bobby helped Jim Clanton to his feet, he turned to the crowd and announced that there better not be any more disruptions. The sheriff told Mr. Langford that he could continue with the auction.

Using the microphone attached to his truck, Michael Langford said that Mr. Jim Clanton had the high bid of $850 per acre. I watched as Michael paced in front of the crowd of bidders and said, "The bid is $850. Who will give me $875?"

The crowd was once again quiet, with no one bidding. I watched the folks from town and from the mountain strain to get a better look at Jim Clanton. I could almost hear them thinking, *I wonder if that feller from Ohio would pay me $850 an acre for my place?*

Just then, Michael asked the bidders, "Are we all in? Are we all done? Going once, going twice, sold to Mr. Jim Clanton from Ohio."

There was a lot of mumbling from the mountain folks as they headed to their trucks to go home. I heard several of them say, talking about Jim Clanton, "Who is this guy, anyway?"

When the crowd dwindled to just a few, Jim Clanton walked down to the mailbox where Michael Langford was. Michael shook hands with him and congratulated him on the purchase of Turkey Holler's place. I noticed that Jim Clanton's left eye was already beginning to turn black as Michael apologized for the actions of Billy Barr.

Mr. Clanton told Michael not to think anything of it, and that it certainly wasn't his fault. Then he turned to Sheriff Bobby Spillman and told him to get Billy Barr out of the car and to take the handcuffs off him.

The sheriff asked Jim Clanton if he was crazy and said that he could keep Billy in jail for a long time. "That way, we won't have any more trouble out of Billy Barr," said the sheriff.

Jim Clanton told the sheriff to do what he said and let Billy Barr free. Then he told Michael that he would wire the money into Michael's trust account before noon on Monday.

Michael said he would have his attorney draw up the deed for Turkey Holler's place, and that Hattie would sign everything before noon on Monday.

I watched as the sheriff opened the back door of his truck, yanked Billy Barr out, and slammed him up against the rear fender. The sheriff took the handcuffs off and told Billy to go home, and that he better not cause any more trouble.

Jim Clanton and the sheriff turned the truck around and headed down the mountain and back toward town. Michael Langford strolled up to the front porch and congratulated Hattie on the sale of her mama's place. Michael then asked Mike Wall to help drive the bidders back to his office. As he was leaving, Michael told Hattie that once he got everybody back to town, he would come up to my place to visit.

After Mr. Langford and Mike drove away, Charlie, Hattie, and I started toward Charlie's old truck for the short ride home. Just as Hattie reached for the handle on the truck, Frail Jones jumped out from behind one of the trees where Charlie had parked.

Hattie screamed and almost fell as Frail shouted that this land was rightfully his, and that her daddy had cheated his father out of it. He yelled that this wasn't over by a long shot, and that he would own the land one way or another.

Charlie opened his door, reached under the seat, and grabbed his pistol. He pointed the pistol at Frail and yelled for him to get the hell away from us.

I heard Frail cussing as he turned and walked toward his property and the fire tower.

Hattie was trembling as she got in the backseat of Charlie's truck. Charlie put his pistol back under the front seat and watched Frail until he was completely out of sight. When

Charlie got behind the wheel, he turned to Hattie and said, "Don't mind Frail none. I knew his sorry-ass daddy, and I've known Frail all his life, and both of them are so full of crap their eyes are brown."

When we drove down the mountain toward home, I couldn't help noticing that Hattie was quiet. I turned in my seat, looked at her, and asked if she was all right. As the tears begin to flow, Hattie said she was sad because she would probably never see her mama's home again. All I could say was to tell her that everything was going to be all right. When she came to my house to visit, we would get Charlie to bring us back to her mama's place for a look-see.

I then tried to change the subject and told Charlie that it would be suppertime before long, and we should just drive on to Moravian Falls to get something to eat.

Charlie said that was a great idea, and that he had been fish-hungry all week. He said, "You know, that Moravian Café has fried flounder, shrimp, hushpuppies, and coleslaw on their menu every Friday and Saturday night." Charlie asked Hattie if she liked fish and shrimp, and Hattie said they were one of her favorite meals.

Soon, we pulled into the parking lot of the café. Charlie said, "I'm a little short on cash. Dessie, do you mind picking up supper?"

That's when Hattie spoke up from the backseat and announced to Charlie that it was her treat. She said it was the least she could do after all the trouble we had gone through to help with her mama's place. Then she added, "Besides, I'm now $69,275 richer, except I still owe Michael Langford his fees."

It wasn't long before the whole truck smelled like fried fish as we drove through Moravian Falls and headed back up the mountain toward home. When we drove over the bridge at the Noah Hole and past Mike Wall's cabin, I noticed Mike's truck parked in his driveway. We continued up the winding road. As we passed Billy Barr's trailer, I saw that he had taken Sheriff Bobby Spillman's advice and gone home. His old truck was parked down in the holler, and all the lights were on in the trailer. *I couldn't help thinking, Billy sure showed Jim Clanton what's what. All it took was one blow from a mountain man to knock a prissy Yankee on his ass.*

Soon, we passed by Ken Martin's orchard and Preacher Wright's house, and I noticed that they had already gotten back home from the auction. I couldn't help thinking that it would have been nice if Mr. Martin bought Turkey Holler's place. He could have expanded his apple orchard business and hired more mountain folks to work. Hob and I both used to help Ken pick his apples in season. He was a good neighbor as well as a good friend.

When we rounded the final curve in the mountain road headed for my home, I saw Michael Langford's truck parked at my mailbox. I turned to Hattie and said, "I told you Michael is a man of his word. He said he would be up to visit, and there he is sitting on the front porch."

CHAPTER NINETEEN

Michael stood up from his rocking chair and waited while we approached the steps to the front porch. Charlie went on ahead of us and into the house to put all those bags of fish on the kitchen table. Hattie Mae held tight to my arm as she helped me up the steps and into my favorite rocking chair. Michael started to speak, but Hattie cut him off and said, "Before you begin, I want to apologize for what happened at your auction today. I'm just terribly embarrassed, and I am truly sorry."

Michael said, "Was that not the craziest thing you've ever seen? However, it wasn't the first fight that's broken out at one of my auctions, and I'm sure it won't be the last. Forget about the fight. I'm still in shock that the property brought $850 per acre, and that Jim Clanton made Sheriff Bobby let Billy Barr go free."

Charlie opened the screen door and said, "Now, that was real smart for Jim Clanton to make the sheriff let Billy go. Not many, if any, on this mountain care anything for Billy Barr. In fact, most people can't stand him. But he's from the mountain, and not from Ohio. If Jim Clanton is looking to buy up land here on the mountain and in Moravian, then he's smart to not upset these old country folks."

Michael spoke up and said, "If you look at it that way, Charlie, I guess he was smart to let Billy go." Then he turned toward Hattie and told her that Mr. Clanton was going to wire the money for the sale before noon on Monday. He said that after he received the wire transfer, he would call her to come down to his office to sign all the papers. Once the papers were signed, Michael said he would give Hattie a certified check for her proceeds and a copy of the closing documents.

I said, "Michael, won't you stay and eat with us? We bought enough fish and all the fixings to feed half of Wilkes County."

Michael said that if our supper came from the Moravian Café, it would be the best flounder we'd ever eaten.

Charlie said, "Dessie, help me get all this food out onto the porch while Hattie and Michael visit." I got up from my comfortable rocker and followed Charlie into the kitchen. He told me that if I got the dishes, he would get the coffee table and the food and move them onto the front porch.

I asked Charlie if I should tell Michael about the visit we had from old man Buford from the funeral parlor, and how Jim Clanton and Sheriff Bobby were going to try to pin Lou's death on Buford unless he convinced me to sell my place. I told Charlie I was also going to tell Michael that they threatened Hamp with prison. The sheriff claimed he would pin Turkey Holler's death on Hamp if he didn't sell his land to Jim Clanton.

Charlie said, "Dessie, you should not tell Michael or anyone else about Buford, Hamp, Lou, or Turkey Holler Bill. We need to just let things settle down, and maybe this old mountain and all the folks living here can get back to normal. Besides, we don't know who is in cahoots with the sheriff or with Jim Clanton."

When we gathered up the food and all the dishes, we returned to the front porch, where Hattie and Michael were waiting on supper. Soon, we had eaten every single piece of flounder and all the hushpuppies. The only food left was two big batches of French fries and some coleslaw that Charlie said he would take to his place to feed to his chickens.

Just then, the phone rang. Hattie jumped from her chair and said she would get it. I heard her say, "Hello, Mike." And then, "That would be great. See you then." She returned to the porch and said, "That was Mike Wall on the phone, and he said he'll come pick us up in the morning for church."

Michael Langford said he should be going, and that he, too, would see us tomorrow at church. I watched as he got into his truck and headed back down the mountain.

Charlie said, "You know, Dessie, after this crazy day and all the fussing and fighting, it might be best if I stay the night, just to be on the safe side." He said that he would just pile up on the couch and wouldn't be a bother to Hattie and me.

Charlie then walked down to his truck and opened the toolbox in the back and got out a quart jar of white lightning. When he returned to his rocking chair, he asked Hattie if she wanted a sip of that powerful shine. Hattie just smiled while making an awful face and shaking her head in a definite no.

Charlie said, "Hattie, I'll tell you what your mama used to say about shine. She would say, 'Ah, take a little drink. It won't hurt you.' White liquor has made me a lot of money, but has also got me into a lot of trouble."

Hattie asked Charlie if his liquor still had ever been raided or blown up by the sheriff or federal revenuers.

"Lord no, Hattie. That crooked sheriff Bobby Spillman is one of my biggest customers," answered Charlie. He added that after he made his monthly liquor runs across the mountain, he always made sure that the revenuers were well paid.

Hattie said, "Well, Charlie, you said that making and drinking white liquor got you into a lot of trouble. Sounds like to me you've made a good living making the stuff."

Charlie looked at Hattie as he took a big sip out of the quart jar and said, "Hattie, white liquor is made for selling, and not for drinking. That's where all my problems are. I like drinking it more than selling it and making money." Charlie then turned to me and said, "Dessie, you remember when we were just teenagers and the carnival came to Moravian, and how all of us were so excited and wanted to go?"

Our mama and daddy told us we couldn't go, and that the carnival was of the devil because of the sideshows they had. I remember it only cost a dime to get in, and that included being able to ride all the rides. They had a merry-go-round, a small Ferris wheel, a wood roller coaster, and a round, tall tower that had swings attached with real long chains. The faster around the tower went, the faster and higher the swings went. The swings got so high you could see all of Moravian Falls. They also had tents, and for just a nickel more you could go in to see the tallest man or the shortest woman. And they even had what we called the "Hoochie-Coochie Tent." It cost a dime to get into the Hoochie-Coochie Tent, because that's where beautiful women played loud music and took all their clothes off. They called those women strippers.

Hattie said, "Charlie, I bet you went to the carnival, and I also bet you went into the Hoochie-Coochie Tent."

Charlie said, "Well, not exactly, Hattie. My friend Chester who lived in Moravian borrowed his daddy's truck under the pretense that he and I were going down to the New River to catch catfish all night. I was about the only friend Chester had. He was only sixteen years old and weighted well over three hundred pounds and pretty much kept to himself.

"Chester drove up the mountain and picked me up, but

instead of going fishing, we headed straight toward the carnival. Halfway down the mountain, we stopped by old man Brock's liquor still and got us two pint jars of white lightning. We were about half lit by the time we got to the carnival. We paid our dime to get in and just walked around and marveled at all the rides and the sideshow tents. We finally made our way to the Hoochie-Coochie Tent, where there were beautiful women dancing on stage. After their dance, they announced to all the men watching that if they wanted to see a lot more, it cost a dime to go inside the tent for the rest of the show.

"Chester and I both wanted to go into the Hoochie-Coochie Tent but were afraid that if our mamas found out, it would be hell to pay. We decided that if they found out we went to the carnival and just rode the rides, they would be mad, but at least they wouldn't kill us. We decided to ride the tower with the swings that was located right beside all the tents.

"There was a long line of folks waiting to get on the high swing ride. Chester and I got in line and watched as the swings started off slowly, moving around in a circle. Then the swings began to speed up, getting faster and faster, and the riders were getting higher and higher. The folks riding were laughing and screaming all at the same time.

"Finally, it was our turn to get on our very first carnival ride. Chester was so excited. Because of his size, he had trouble getting seated into his swing. One of the carnival workers came over and with a lot of work managed to squeeze Chester into his seat. I took the swing behind Chester and watched as the ride slowly began moving in a circle. It began to get faster and faster. The faster the swing got, the higher we got. Soon, we were at the top of the ride and so far off the ground that I could see all of town. Then, with a loud pop and a scream, I watched as the chains on Chester's swing broke, throwing him, swing and all, through the Hoochie-Coochie Tent. The tent collapsed, and I watched as naked, screaming women tried to beat poor old Chester to death.

"Chester was bruised up a bit, and when word got back to his mama, he could not convince her that he didn't go in the Hoochie-Coochie Tent. He tried his best to tell her that he had no choice, that he was thrown into the tent. Chester later told me that his mama made him go to the apple orchard and cut a switch. He said that was the worst whooping he ever got."

Hattie burst out laughing. I had heard that story from Charlie at least a hundred times, but it was still funny. I said my good nights and left Hattie and Charlie still talking on the front porch.

Mary said, "Miss Dessie, this is a good place to stop for a potty break, and I need to get another notebook as well. I can hardly wait to write this article for my paper. Maybe I should write it as a series and put your picture on the front page. We would have to think of a catchy title to attract more readers. What do you think, Dessie?"

I told Mary, "I think we need to get on with the story. I don't want to stay up all night. And there would be no pictures."

Mary got a fresh notebook and pen and said, "I'm ready, Miss Dessie. Let's continue."

CHAPTER TWENTY

The next morning, I woke up to the smell of frying bacon and the sound of Charlie singing "White Lightning" by George Jones. That was Charlie's favorite song, and he sang it every morning when he fixed his breakfast.

I got dressed for church before I went into the kitchen. Hattie had also gotten ready for church and was sitting at the table sipping a cup of coffee.

Charlie set the food on the table—bacon, scrambled eggs, biscuits, and my favorite, milk gravy made with bacon grease. Charlie said, "Dessie, while you and Hattie are at church, I'm going home to check on my still. You know how those old redneck boys like to mess with somebody else's still." Charlie chuckled. "Heck, I guess I'm one of those old redneck boys. What do you think, Hattie?"

Hattie said, "Well, Charlie, you're my favorite redneck of all time."

After breakfast, I started to clean the kitchen when Hattie said, "Dessie, would you and Charlie get your coffee and come and sit at the table? I have something to talk to y'all about."

I finished putting the dishes in the sink, poured myself a fresh cup of coffee, and sat back down at the kitchen table.

Hattie said, "I stayed awake last night thinking about my mama, Lou, and the two of you, and I decided that I want to pay for Lou's funeral." Hattie held my hand. "Now, before you say no, let me explain. I don't have anybody back home in Georgia, and y'all are the only family I have left. Monday, I'm going to get paid a lot of money, and I can't think of a better way to spend some of it. What do y'all think?"

Charlie was the first to speak. "Since Lou left me her place, I thought I would eventually sell it and take care of the expense of her funeral. However, if that's what you want to do, I guess it's all right with me." He said, "Your mama would be really proud of you, Hattie. What do you think, Dessie?"

Tears began to fill my eyes as I hugged Hattie. I whispered, "I love you, Hattie."

Hattie jumped up from the table, headed toward the sink, and said, "Well, that's that. Now, let's get these dishes washed and put away. Mike will be here to pick us up in a few minutes. After church, maybe Mike will take us by the funeral parlor so we can make the final arrangements for Lou's funeral, and I'll tell old man Buford what we decided."

It wasn't long after the last dish was put away when I heard the sound of a vehicle making its way up the old mountain road. Hattie, Charlie, and I went onto the front porch as Mike parked his truck down by my mailbox.

Mike said, "Good morning, ladies. Don't y'all look pretty on this beautiful morning."

Mike was always so sweet to me, and I considered him a great friend. He was the only man I knew that wore a suit and tie at the Moravian Falls Baptist Church. All the men of the church, even the preacher, usually wore overalls or jeans with a long-sleeved shirt.

Charlie helped me into the backseat of Mike's truck and, as he was closing the door, said, "I'm off to check things at my place. I'll be back before dark."

Mike rolled down his window and said, "Charlie, don't worry. I'll take good care of these ladies."

On the way down the mountain, I asked Mike if he would mind taking Hattie and me over to the funeral parlor to meet with old man Buford.

Mike said, "Miss Dessie, I don't have a thing to do today except visit with the Lord and do whatever you ladies need done. You know I don't mind taking you and Hattie anywhere you need to go."

It seemed like only a few minutes before we pulled into the church parking lot. Several people were standing around talking while others made their way into the sanctuary. It was such a beautiful day. The children were running around in the churchyard, wanting to play more than to attend a sermon. I thought, *How innocent these babies are, and how I love to see them in God's house! I wish I could see God's plan and what He has in store for all these lovely children.*

My thoughts were interrupted when Beulah began playing "Amazing Grace" on the old church organ. Miss Beulah had lived in Moravian Falls her entire life, never married, and devoted all her time to church activities. Her daddy used to own the Apple Co-op down in Moravian. He died a few years back, and rumor had it that he left her over one million dollars in his will. After he was dead and buried, Miss Beulah had lots of suitors, but she never paid them any mind.

After Preacher Wright's service was over, Hattie and I waited for Buford at the foot of the church steps. When he finally quit talking to all his friends, he came down the steps and hugged Hattie like he had known her forever.

I told Buford, "I know you don't like to work on Sunday, but since we're in town, would you mind if we stop by your funeral parlor to make Lou's final arrangements?"

Buford said that wasn't a problem, as he had already figured we would want the same service for Lou that we had for Turkey Holler Bill. Buford said, "I'll be there in ten minutes. See you then."

Mike escorted Hattie and me to his truck and asked, "Ladies, after you meet with Buford, would y'all let me buy your lunch at the café?"

Hattie quickly spoke up and said, "That would be great, Mike. Dessie and I didn't want to cook today anyway."

Mike just smiled as we pulled out of the parking lot and onto Highway 16 toward the funeral parlor.

Buford got there before us. His truck was parked directly in front of the building. Mike helped Hattie and me out of the truck and opened the front door of the funeral parlor for us. As the door was closing, Mike turned and headed back toward his truck. I opened the door and asked Mike, "Where are you going?"

Mike said, "I thought what y'all have to talk about is none of my business, and that it should be just for the family."

I said, "Mike, you're family to me."

Mike just smiled and followed Hattie and me back into the office, where Buford was sitting at his desk.

Buford said that he planned to give Lou a burial similar to the one that Hattie's mama had.

I asked him if Lou could be buried beside her sister, Turkey Holler Bill, and said that I wanted a closed casket. I also told Buford that I wanted the same flowers that he had for Ida's funeral.

Buford then reached into his desk drawer and brought out a blank invoice. At the top, he wrote my name, and in the description, he wrote, "Burial service for Lou Adams." Then, at the bottom of the invoice, Buford noted the cost, forty-six hundred dollars, and handed it over with a pen for me to sign.

While I was signing the invoice, Buford said, "Dessie, you and Charlie can pay me a hundred dollars a month, and I won't charge you any interest. That way, the bill will be paid in full in about four years."

Hattie spoke up and said, "Mr. Buford, I will be paying cash for Aunt Lou's service, and I'll have the money to you by next Wednesday. Sharing the money from the sale of Mama's place is the least I can do for my family."

I asked Buford how soon he could have everything ready, and when he thought we could lay poor old Lou to rest.

Buford said he could have Lou ready for burial by Wednesday. He thought the service would be best if it was held around two o'clock, which would allow time for the flowers to be set in place.

I told Buford that I really appreciated all he had done for Turkey Holler Bill and for Lou. I thanked him for being so kind to Charlie, Hattie, and me and said that we considered him a good friend.

Just as the three of us walked out of his office and back to the main lobby of the funeral parlor, we were greeted by Sheriff Bobby Spillman and Jim Clanton.

Sheriff Bobby asked me if Buford was in his office, and if anyone else was in the building.

"Buford is in his office, and he's by himself, as far as I know," I said.

Sheriff Bobby Spillman said he was sorry for my loss, and that he hoped to see me soon.

Not if I can help it, I thought.

CHAPTER TWENTY-ONE

◆

Mike had trouble finding a place to park at the Moravian Café. It looked like everyone at church had the same idea of not cooking lunch at home. After Mike parked the truck, he went inside the café and put our name on the waiting list. There was a big old hickory nut tree in the yard of the café with benches placed neatly underneath. Hattie and I found us a comfortable seat until our name was called for lunch.

"The lady inside said it would only be about a ten-minute wait until we can be seated," Mike said as he joined us on the bench.

Hattie said, "Well, it's Sunday, and I'm going to order fried chicken, mashed potatoes, peas, biscuits, and a large glass of iced tea. That's what everybody should eat for lunch on Sunday."

Mike agreed and then said, "I wonder what the sheriff and Jim Clanton wanted with Buford, and especially why the sheriff asked if there was anyone else in the building."

Leaning close and in a low voice, I told Mike that when we got back home, I would explain what I thought was happening between Bobby Spillman, Jim Clanton, and Buford. I said, "There are too many people around for us to talk about this now."

Just then, the lady in the café announced over the loudspeaker, "Mike Wall, your table for three is ready."

After we got to the table and sipped on sweet tea, Mike and Hattie both ordered fried chicken with all the fixings. I ordered the same, but I remembered that Charlie thought the Moravian Café made the best cheeseburgers he had ever eaten, so I added that to my order as well. There was no way I could eat that much food, so I had them wrap up my fried chicken with all the fixings to take home.

When we got back home, I saw that Charlie had parked his truck in the front yard and was sitting in his favorite rocking chair on the porch. When we were out of the truck, I told Charlie I had brought him fried chicken for lunch from the Moravian Café.

Charlie smiled and said, "Thanks, Dessie. I really wish you had brought me a couple of their cheeseburgers instead."

I got onto the porch and had just sat down when the phone rang inside the house. Charlie said, "That dang phone has been ringing off and on for the last thirty minutes."

Hattie said, "I'll get it," and went in the house. The screen door slammed shut, and I heard her say, "Hello, Mr. Buford. Yes, Dessie is sitting on the front porch. I'll tell her you want to talk to her."

Hattie returned to the porch and told me that Mr. Buford said it was urgent. Charlie helped me to my feet and held the screen door open for me.

Buford said to me in a panicked voice that Sheriff Bobby Spillman and Jim Clanton had come into his office right after we left. The sheriff told him that he saw Mike's truck in the parking lot and figured I was there meeting with him. Jim Clanton wanted to know if he had talked to me about selling my place to him. Then the sheriff pulled out his pistol and laid it on the desk and told Buford that if he didn't do exactly what they said, that if I didn't sell to Jim Clanton, he would make things real bad for Buford and his family.

Buford asked the sheriff how he was supposed to talk me into selling, and said that I had a mind of my own. He told Jim Clanton that if they would leave him and his family alone, he would sell his home and funeral parlor to them. Jim Clanton just laughed and told him he didn't want his home or business. Besides, he said, more dead people might turn up, and someone would need to bury them.

Buford told me that he was going to call his friend in the governor's office first thing in the morning. "I'm going to tell him what's going on up here with that crooked Bobby Spillman and Jim Clanton. After I talk to my friend, I'll call you back and let you know what his advice was. Dessie, I'm scared to death."

Buford then gave me quite a shock when he said, "Dessie, I needed to buy more time. Please forgive me. I told them that's why you and Hattie were in my office, to talk to me about selling. I also told them that I talked to Mike Wall about selling his place to Jim Clanton. Dessie, I'm sorry. I needed more time. I told them that both you and Mike are thinking seriously about it. If those two crooks stop by your place, please lie and tell them that we talked, and that you're thinking about it. Tell Mike, too."

I thought, Boy, that's just great. Now he's brought my good friend Mike Wall into all the crazy mess with the sheriff and Jim Clanton.

Buford said that as soon as Lou's funeral was over, he and his family were leaving town. He said he was going to Raleigh until all this mess blew over, or until his friend at the governor's office figured out what to do. He ended the phone call by saying, "Dessie, y'all be safe. I just know something terrible is going to happen."

After I hung up the phone, I just stood there thinking about what I was going to tell Charlie and Mike when I went back to the porch.

As I opened the screen door, the first thing I noticed was that Charlie had finished every piece of the fried chicken I brought home. Only the bones were left in the Styrofoam box.

Hattie, Mike, and Charlie were all drinking sweet tea and just visiting.

I sat down in my rocking chair and said, "I need to talk to y'all about something real serious."

Mike said, "Dessie, are you okay? You're so pale, you look like you might faint."

"I just got off the phone with Buford. He told me he had a disturbing visit from Sheriff Bobby Spillman and Jim Clanton," I said. I then explained to Mike that Buford had visited with me just the other night, and he said that the sheriff and Jim Clanton had come by the funeral parlor right after Lou was shot. Buford claimed that the sheriff said he would pin Lou's murder on him if he didn't try to convince me to sell Jim Clanton my place.

I went on to tell Mike and Charlie that when we left the funeral parlor after church, the sheriff and Jim Clanton cornered Buford in his office and asked if he had talked to me about selling. Buford said the sheriff even pulled his pistol in an effort to threaten him into doing what he demanded. Buford was scared. He said he just wanted to get out of there. In an effort to get them to leave him be, Buford told them we were there to talk about Lou's funeral arrangements. He told them that we also discussed selling my place to Jim Clanton. "Buford was so scared that he said he not only talked to me, but also to you, Mike," I said. "He told Sheriff Bobby and Jim Clanton that we both are seriously considering selling our places to Jim Clanton."

Mike stood up and said, "I already told them there's no way I'll be selling, especially to them. I guess I'll need to leave my gun case unlocked and put my old .45 under my pillow for a while."

"Buford said that right after Lou's funeral, he's taking his whole family and leaving town," I said. "He also said that he's going to call his friend in the governor's office first thing in the morning and ask for advice on what to do."

Before anyone else said anything, Hattie asked if she could use my phone and went back into the house.

I know my brother Charlie better than anyone, and when I looked at him, I could see the anger in his face and the fire in his eyes. Charlie said, "Dessie, I'm staying with you until this crap is settled one way or another. Don't worry. I'll sleep on the couch with your old pump shotgun, and if anyone, including the sheriff, comes around this place, I'll fill his ass with buckshot."

I told Charlie I was worried, and that maybe we should call somebody and ask for help.

Charlie said, "We're mountain folk, and we'll handle this ourselves. Besides, who are you going to call? Bobby is the law on this mountain. It's best if we take matters into our own hands."

Mike said, "Charlie and Dessie, if you need me, call me. I'm just at the foot of this mountain, and me and my guns can be here in no time. It might be best if I come and pick up Dessie and Hattie for Lou's funeral Wednesday. If we travel separately from Charlie, they'll be less likely to confront us."

I watched Mike's taillights as he slowly made his way down the road and out of sight.

With anger still on his face and in his eyes, Charlie said, "Dessie, you best get in the house. I'll be in shortly to make sure everything is locked up."

When I walked into my bedroom, I looked out the window to a full moon shining on my old mountain home. I thought, *I wish my Hob was here. He would know exactly what to do.*

CHAPTER TWENTY-TWO

I must have been very tired. It was almost nine o'clock before I woke up Monday morning. Hattie had already made coffee, and she and Charlie were sitting at the kitchen table. Hattie had prepared a big country breakfast of fried eggs, fried sausage, grits, and fresh biscuits. She asked if she could fix me a plate and get me a cup of coffee.

I said, "I think I'll just have a sausage biscuit and a cup of coffee." I asked Hattie what time she needed to go to Michael Langford's office to close on the sale of her mama's place.

Hattie said that Mr. Langford told her he would call when he received the payment from Jim Clanton. Then all she would have to do was drive to the office, sign the papers, and pick up a check from Michael.

"Dessie, I have a great idea," said Hattie. "When Mr. Langford calls, why don't you ride with me to town, and we can do some grocery shopping. We're completely out of milk and are running low on bread, cornmeal, coffee, and a few other things."

I said, "Hattie, that's very sweet of you, but today is Monday, and Mike Wall always comes on the first Monday of the month to take me grocery shopping, and on the way home we stop by the egg lady to buy a couple dozen."

Hattie said, "Come on, Dessie. I'll call Mike and tell him you and I are going to town for groceries, and that you'll see him next Monday. Besides, I haven't met Miss April, and I have never bought eggs from anyplace except the grocery store. I want to see what it's like to buy eggs right out of the chicken."

I just smiled and told Hattie that we would make a girls' day out of it. I was sure Mike had more important things to do anyway.

It was just a little while after Hattie called Mike Wall that Michael Langford called to let her know that he had received the wire transfer from Jim Clanton. Hattie told Michael that she and I were getting ready to go to town, and that we should be at his office within the hour.

Soon, we were in Hattie's car and headed down the mountain to Michael Langford's office. When we passed Mr. Martin's home and apple orchard, I couldn't help noticing that there were a lot of cars and trucks parked in his drive and even in his front yard. I said to Hattie, "I hope everything is okay at Mr. Martin's place. The only time there are that many cars and trucks at his orchard is when it's apple-picking time, and we're far from picking time. I think we should stop by on our way back up the mountain, just to make sure everything is fine there."

Right before we got to Billy Barr's place, I heard a shotgun blast coming from the direction of his old trailer. When we got around the curve, I looked down the mountain toward Billy's and saw him standing in his side yard holding his shotgun. I watched as Billy moved around to the back of a big hickory nut tree growing in his yard. Hattie slowed down just enough for me to watch Billy bend over and pick up a dead squirrel lying under the tree.

"I guess that's old Billy's supper," Hattie said.

"Probably so," I said, laughing. "At least he ain't shooting at us."

When we passed Mike Wall's place, I saw that his truck was not in the driveway. I thought, Mike is probably glad that he doesn't have to take me to the store today. *I'm sure he has plenty of errands to run for himself, or he's out figuring what he's going to do about Sheriff Bobby Spillman and Jim Clanton. I know Mike Wall, and he ain't going to just roll over and give in. He'll fight if necessary.*

It wasn't long before we turned onto Highway 16 headed toward Wilkesboro and Michael Langford's office. During the drive, I told Hattie that once we got to Michael's office, I thought I would just stay in the car while she closed on the sale of her mama's land. I said, "Hattie, this is between you and Michael Langford, and it's none of my business regarding how much money you're getting, so I think I'll feel more comfortable sitting in the car."

Hattie said she didn't mind at all if I knew everything about her, and that included the money, but if it made me more comfortable, it would be okay.

I had waited about thirty minutes when the front door of Michael's office opened and Hattie came out, heading for her car. When she got in, she said, "Dessie, what is the largest amount of money you have ever held in your hands?"

I said, "That would be forty-six hundred dollars. That was the amount old Lou brought to my house when your mama died. She had all those hundred-dollar bills stuffed in her overalls and rubber boots to pay old man Buford for your mama's funeral."

I watched as Hattie's eyes filled with tears, and I thought, *That was stupid. Hattie was so excited, and I just stole her thunder.*

Hattie said, "I will be forever grateful for Aunt Lou and what she did for her sister and my mama. Dessie, do you know the best bank where I can open up an account and deposit all this money?"

I said, "As a matter of fact, I do. My son Don Pennell just happens to be the branch manager of Wilkes Central Bank." I told her his branch was located just outside Wilkesboro on Highway 16 next to the Dairy Queen.

Hattie said she remembered Don from the day that her mama was buried. She said she introduced herself to Don and Bill after Charlie came to the house drunk. She remembered how Don, Bill, and Hamp laughed when Charlie told Dorothy that, no higher up than he was, he didn't have too far to fall. "I'll never forget that as long as I live," added Hattie.

We both were still laughing when we pulled into the parking lot of the Wilkes Central Bank. While still sitting in the car, Hattie told me that eighty-one and a half acres at $850 per acre totaled $69,275, less eight percent for Michael's fee, which made her check amount $63,733.00.

Hattie and I went into the bank and asked one of the tellers if Don Pennell was available. She told us to take a seat and she would inquire if Mr. Pennell could meet with us. We sat in the bank lobby as the nice young lady went down the hall and into Don's office. It was only a few seconds before Don came into the lobby and said, "Mom, what are y'all doing here? Is everything all right?"

Hattie stood up and said, "Don, there is nothing wrong. Dessie and I are here to open up an account and make a deposit."

Don looked relieved when he knew there was nothing terribly wrong, and that he had a new customer named Hattie Mae. He asked us to follow him to discuss the best way to open

Hattie's account. Once we got into Don's office, Hattie handed him the pile of papers Michael Langford had given her, along with the check.

Once Don saw the amount of the check, he asked, "Hattie, do you have any major purchases coming up soon?"

Hattie said, "I promised Mr. Buford that I would stop by today and pay $4,600 for Aunt Lou's funeral. Other than just doing a little shopping, that's all the money I need access to."

Don said, "Then I would suggest that we put $13,733.00 into a regular checking account and the balance of $50,000 into a savings account so you can earn some interest."

Hattie agreed. When all the paperwork was done, we said our goodbyes to Don and left the bank. We then drove straight to the funeral parlor to pay Buford for Lou's funeral.

When we got there, I noticed that Buford's car was not in the parking lot. Hattie and I went in and were met by a nice young lady that told us Buford had called and said he was a little under the weather and would not be in today. Hattie wrote the check, gave it to the lady, and asked for a receipt.

Once we got back into Hattie's car, she said, "Well, Dessie, all our chores are done. Now, where shall we begin our shopping spree?"

Hattie and I visited several small shops in Moravian Falls,

where she bought some shoes and clothes. We had a hot dog lunch at the Woolworths five-and-dime before we went grocery shopping. As usual, a group of old farmers was sitting in straight-back chairs around the entrance of the grocery store. They sat there every day chewing tobacco, drinking Cokes, and talking about everything and everybody in Wilkes County.

As we approached the group, one of the old men, Delmar, said, "Dessie, I was sure sorry to hear the sad news about Lou." In the same breath, he asked, "Who is this lovely lady with you?"

I said, "This is Hattie Mae. She is Turkey Holler Bill's daughter from Georgia."

Delmar stood up, removed his old Braves baseball hat, shook Hattie's hand, and told her how sorry he was to hear the news about her mama.

Hattie and I went into the grocery store and bought enough supplies to last at least a week. When we started out of the store, the same group of old men was still sitting out front. All of them were laughing like crazy and choking on chewing tobacco and Coke.

Delmar finally caught his breath and said, "We were laughing about Lou's husband, Hank, and the Christmas present he sent her when he was in the army."

Hattie said, "Oh, you're talking about the two sticks of chewing gum he sent to Lou in a Santa Christmas card."

Delmar answered that they were talking about the exotic bird Hank sent Lou and the family.

I said, "Delmar, Hattie don't need to hear that stupid story. We're getting short on time and need to get these groceries home."

Hattie said, "Oh, Dessie, I just have to hear that Christmas story about Lou and Hank."

One of the old men stood and said, "Hattie, take my seat."

Hattie sat down, and Delmar began. All the others guys started snickering, even though they had just heard the story while we were in the store.

Delmar said, "It was close to Christmas, and Hank took his entire army paycheck and went to the closest city, which was San Francisco. He was looking for just the right gift for Lou. While Hank was shopping, he just happened to walk into a pet store that sold all kinds of animals, including birds. Story has it that Hank spent his entire paycheck and bought Lou a huge exotic talking bird. Hank had the pet store ship the bird to Lou, and his loving Christmas gift arrived on Christmas Eve.

"Later that year, Hank got his first furlough from the army and headed straight home to his loving wife. After the first day being back home on the mountain, Hank asked Lou where the bird was that he had sent home for Christmas.

"Lou said, 'Hank, what are you talking about? Oh, yeah, I remember. That bird got here on Christmas Eve, and I chopped its head off and plucked it. I took it down to Dessie for her to cook for Christmas dinner. It was delicious and fed the entire family, including all the kids.' Hank got real upset and said, 'Lou, you know you didn't kill that bird.' Lou said, 'Yes, I did, and it was great.' Hank said, 'Lou, that was a real rare and expensive exotic bird. Why, that bird could even speak two languages.' Lou just looked Hank straight in the eye and said, 'Well, hell. Seems like he woulda said something then, don't it?' "

After Hattie and all the good old boys stopped laughing, we loaded up to head home. When we got in the car, Hattie was still laughing. She asked if the story was true. I just smiled and said that was one of the best Christmas dinners we ever had.

CHAPTER TWENTY-THREE

When we started up the mountain toward home, Hattie said, "I almost forgot. We still need to stop by the egg lady's house and buy a couple dozen, fresh from the chickens."

Miss April was throwing out cracked corn that was mixed with chicken feed when we pulled in front of her house. It seemed like there must have been at least four dozen chickens fighting for every piece that hit the ground.

Miss April said, "Dessie, what a nice surprise for you and Hattie to come visit. I was expecting you and that sweet Mike Wall to stop by today for eggs."

Hattie said, "I gave Mr. Mike the day off, and Dessie and I hit the town and shopped for clothes, shoes, and groceries. I think we'll take three dozen of your fresh brown eggs today, Miss April."

April shooed the chickens off her front porch as she went into the house for our eggs. Soon, she returned with three cartons in a brown grocery bag and handed them to Hattie. Miss April said, "Hattie, I just gathered these eggs this morning, and they would be great to use in a cake, being that they're that fresh."

Hattie paid and thanked April for the eggs. But when we

started to walk to the car, April said, "Wait a minute, Dessie. Do you know what's going on up the mountain? There have been a lot of cars and trucks on this old road today."

I told April that when we left this morning, I saw vehicles at Ken Mattin's place, but I didn't know why.

April said, "I'm sure there is nothing dreadfully wrong. I was just curious. Thanks for stopping by, and I'll see y'all next week."

When we drove past Mr. Martin's place, it looked like even more cars and trucks were there than earlier that morning. I told Hattie, "Let's get home and put the groceries away and then ride back down to the Martins' to make sure they're all okay."

It wasn't long before Hattie and I were back in the car, headed to Ken Martin's apple orchard. When we parked and got out, I saw Ken standing in the entrance of his largest barn, which held all his orchard equipment and tractors. Surrounding Ken were thirty or so other men, including his oldest son, Ronnie. Just as we walked up beside Ronnie, I heard Mr. Martin yell, "Sold!" to Mr. Rogers from South Orchard Farm. Then Ken announced to the crowd, "That was the last big piece of equipment I have to sell for today. Michael Langford will be selling all the small equipment in a couple of weeks."

As the crowd of men began to leave, Mr. Martin saw Hattie and me standing with Ronnie. Ken pulled off his ball cap, walked over to me, and, with tears in his eyes, gave me a big mountain-man hug. I was shocked because, over the years I had known him, he had few words to say to me, much less giving me a giant hug. Then he whispered, "Can I walk Hattie and you back to her car so we can talk away from my son?"

I agreed, and as we began to walk toward Hattie's car, Ken said, "Dessie, I have sold all my land and orchards, including the Apple Co-op." He said that he really didn't want to sell, but his son had gotten into some trouble with the law. Ronnie and some of his buddies were making moonshine down past the Noah Hole, and Sheriff Bobby Spillman caught them loading up quart jars of shine in Ronnie's old truck. Ken said, "The sheriff told me that Ronnie is in a heap of trouble, but that he can make this problem go away. All I have to do is sell all my land to Jim Clanton. That crooked Bobby Spillman told me that if I don't sell, he'll see to it that Ronnie gets at least ten years in the federal penitentiary." With tears in his eyes, he said, "I have no choice but to sell, Dessie. I can't let my boy go to prison."

"Where will you go, Ken?" I asked.

"We will be moving soon to Tallahassee, Florida, to live close to my youngest son, Raeford. Maybe it's time for me to retire anyway. I was hoping I could leave this place to Ronnie, but I guess that will never be," Ken said.

When Ken opened my car door, he gently took me by the

hand and said, "Dessie, you, Charlie, and Hattie need to be careful around those two. Jim Clanton bought Turkey Holler Bill's place, and now mine, and I heard that Preacher Wright is thinking about selling his home. If all that happens, it won't be too many left on this old mountain."

I told Ken I was sad to see him sell and move away, but I understood that he was just trying to save his oldest son. I gave him a hug, and Hattie and I headed up the mountain to my house.

When we parked by the mailbox, I saw Charlie, Hamp, and Mike Wall sitting on the front porch. As Hattie and I got closer, I could see that Charlie had gotten some quart jars of Apple Pie Moonshine from the cellar. It was quickly evident to me that Charlie had a snootful of that "powerful stuff," as he liked to call it. Hamp looked like he had enjoyed a few drinks of it as well.

When Hattie and I sat in our rocking chairs, Charlie handed Hattie a jar of shine and said, "Like your mama used to say, 'Ah, take a little drank. It won't hurt you.' "

Hattie smiled at Charlie while shaking her head.

Hamp spoke up and said, "Since you put it that way, Charlie, don't mind if I do."

Charlie then started to hand the quart jar to Mike but was cut short when Mike said, "No thanks, Charlie. I just came up to check on Dessie, and I have to drive back down this curvy mountain road." He then added, "Oh, Charlie, I met a man at the Moravian Café at lunch today that said you and him were close friends. He said his name was Lane Parrish, and that y'all had run around together back in the day."

Charlie said, "l ain't seen Lane in a long time. He and I used to run around together when we were in school. I was always the smallest one of the boys in our class, and I regularly got my butt beat because I wouldn't bow down to them. Lane was such a great friend that he always had my back, no matter how many or how big the boys were that we fought. Sometimes we both would get whipped, and sometimes we would win, but we always did it together. Over the years, we just kind of drifted apart." Charlie gave me a wink, then said, "I went to making whiskey, and Lane went to college and became an assassin for the FBI. He retired a few years back and returned home here in Moravian."

"I didn't even know that the FBI had assassins working for them. I wonder how he got that terrible job," Mike said.

"Lane came to visit me when he got back home, and I asked him that very question," said Charlie. "Lane said that he mostly just did office work for the FBI, until the assassin job came available in Oklahoma City. Lane applied for the job because it paid nearly forty thousand dollars a year, and he wanted to get out of that boring office work. He said that was almost twice as much as he was making doing fingerprint work.

"Lane told me he was such a good shot from hunting squirrels and such on the mountain that he was confident he could get the job. Lane and his wife moved out to Oklahoma City, where he went to school and training. He said that he was top in his class, along with two others guys. One was from Pennsylvania, and the other was from New York City. The problem was there was only one assassin job available. So the FBI put them through one more test. Lane said the FBI bosses put the three finalists together in one room and gave each one of them a .38 Special revolver. Then the bosses told the three candidates, 'If you're going to be an assassin for the FBI, you must kill whoever you are assigned to kill, without question or hesitation.' The bosses told them their last test was to take the gun and go into the next room and kill whoever was sitting in there.

"Lane said the boy from Pennsylvania went in the side room first and was only there for a second. He came back to where the bosses were, handed them his gun, and left without saying a word. Next, the boy from New York City took his gun and went into the side room and closed the door. Lane said he heard talking, and after about five minutes, the boy from New York came back into the room with the FBI bosses and was crying like a baby. He handed them his gun, and in a crying sob he said,

'There is no way I can kill my wife, the mother of my children.' And he ran out of the room.

"Lane said he took the gun and went into the side room for his final test. His bosses waited, and they heard four shots from Lane's revolver. Then, coming from the side room, the bosses heard loud banging and blood-curdling screams. After a few minutes, things in the room got quiet again, and Lane returned to his bosses. Lane handed them his gun and said, 'Why didn't you tell me there were blanks in the gun? I had to beat her to death with a chair.' "

CHAPTER TWENTY-FOUR

After Hamp stopped chuckling from the Apple Pie Moonshine and Charlie's story, he settled back down in the rocking chair and said, "Dessie, we need to talk."

"Hamp, that sounds serious. Are you okay?" I asked.

"I'm fine, except I was paid another visit yesterday from our sheriff and Jim Clanton," said Hamp. "They were wanting to know if I had made up my mind about selling the place, or if I had chosen to go back to prison for killing Turkey Holler Bill. I told Jim Clanton to get his money ready and I would sell my place to him in five days, and that I didn't want any trouble." Hamp said that crooked Bobby Spillman put his arm around him and told him he had made a wise decision.

Then Hamp handed me a piece of newspaper with a number written in large black letters. He said, "Dessie, this is my friend's telephone number back in Detroit. I'm leaving town until all this crazy stuff is over. I'm not going to sell my place, and I darn sure ain't going back to prison. I plan to go down to Moravian late tomorrow night and hop a freight train headed north. It will be days before that jackleg Bobbie Spillman and Jim Clanton even find out that I'm gone, and even when they do, they'll never find me in Detroit. When things on this old mountain get back to normal, Dessie, will you call me in Detroit? I'll catch the next freight train south and home."

I told Hamp that while he was gone, Charlie and I would visit his place every month or so to make sure everything was in order. I told him I would not call until things got back to normal, or until Bobby Spillman and Jim Clanton were out of the picture.

Almost at the same time, Mike and Hamp said, "What do you mean by 'out of the picture,' Dessie?"

Before I could speak, Charlie said, "Those two crooks are dealing with mountain folks. There is only so much pushing we will take until one or more of us mountain rednecks strike back. I hope it don't come to that, but if we have to, we'll protect our own and what belongs to us." Charlie said that time would tell, and that he thought it was a good idea for Hamp to hide out for a while.

Charlie then turned to Mike and said, "Mike, I need a big favor, if you can. I have to go make a white lightning run to all my customers across the mountain and in Moravian Falls. With all that's going on around here, I need you to stay with Dessie and Hattie for three or four days until I get back. I don't feel comfortable leaving without someone here to look after them. You, Preacher Wright, and Ken Martin are the only ones left on this old mountain that I trust."

Mike said, "It will be my honor to look after these two fine ladies. Don't worry, Charlie. I'll come up right after Lou's funeral and stay until you return."

Mike said it was time he started back down the mountain and asked if he could give Hamp a ride home.

Hamp thanked Mike but said, "If you don't mind, I think I'll just stumble through Dessie's backyard, into the mountain woods, and back into my world."

As Mike's truck was making its way down the mountain, Charlie said, "I think I might have had one too many pieces of Apple Pie Moonshine. I should take a nap." Charlie got up, went into the house, and lay down on the sofa, leaving Hattie and me rocking on the front porch.

"Hattie, I'll go get us a cup of coffee if you want, and we can just sit out here in God's creation and watch the world go to sleep," I said.

I went to the kitchen and got us two cups of hot black coffee. When I returned to the porch, Hattie said, "Dessie, there's a man walking up the road."

I strained my eyes, as it was getting late and the sun was going down, but even in the dim light, I could tell it was Preacher Wright. When he got to my mailbox, he waved at Hattie and me and headed to my front porch.

I said, "Hattie, give Preacher Wright a seat, and I'll get him a cup of coffee."

Preacher Wright said, "No need. Dessie. I just had supper. And besides, I'm not going to take up much of your time."

When Preacher Wright sat down, I could see the serious look on his face and in his eyes. He said, "Dessie, the missus and I have thought long and hard about selling our home and land. When that real nice young Jim Clanton came to visit, we decided that now might be the right time for me to retire. I told Mr. Clanton that the only way I would sell was if I could stay long enough to find another preacher for our church and congregation. Mr. Clanton made us a huge offer for our place, and he even said that after the sale, we could stay in our house for up to six months. We think we'll move to Tennessee to be close to our son. We're going to miss the congregation and the folks on this old mountain, but we'll especially miss you, Dessie."

I said, "Preacher Wright, we will miss y'all as well. You know we love you, and we wish you and your family the very best. At least you won't be moving for six more months, which will give us half of a year to say our goodbyes." Then I asked, "Did you say that when Jim Clanton and Sheriff Bobby Spillman came to make you the offer, they were nice?"

Preacher Wright said, "Mr. Clanton was by himself when he

came to visit. I didn't see Sheriff Spillman."

I said, "Every time that I see Jim Clanton, he always has Sheriff Bobby Spillman with him." I told Preacher Wright that I didn't understand why, unless it was for protection from these old mountain folks.

Preacher Wright stood up and said, "I don't know why a man as nice as Jim Clanton would need any protection. I hope you and Hattie have a nice evening. I'll see you at poor old Lou's funeral."

CHAPTER TWENTY-FIVE

The next morning, Hattie and I were sitting at the breakfast table when Charlie came into the kitchen looking for a cup of black coffee. I said, "Charlie, I think you might have had one too many pieces of Apple Pie Moonshine. Your eyes look like two firebricks in a snowstorm."

Hattie couldn't help snickering, but Charlie just grunted as he sat down at the table. I took him a cup of coffee and asked if he wanted some breakfast.

Charlie said, "Who can eat in this kind of shape? I'm just drinking coffee this morning."

After Charlie's third cup, I said, "Hattie and I stopped at Ken Martin's yesterday on our way home, and Ken told me he's selling his orchard and all his land to Jim Clanton. He said that his boy Ronnie got caught running a moonshine still down past the Noah Hole. Sheriff Bobby Spillman told Ken that he can make all Ronnie's trouble go away. All Ken has to do is sell out to Jim Clanton. The sheriff told Ken that if he doesn't sell his land, he'll see to it that Ronnie gets ten years in the federal penitentiary."

Charlie said he had heard that Ronnie and some other boys on the mountain had cranked up a moonshine still. He had planned to talk to Ronnie the next time he saw him, to make sure that he paid off all the right people to stay out of trouble. Charlie added, "Boy, I hate to see Ken and his family move off this old mountain. They sure are good neighbors."

I said, "Charlie, Preacher Wright came to visit with me right after you went to bed yesterday evening, and he's decided to sell his place to Jim Clanton as well. He said that Jim Clanton is one of the nicest men he's ever met. Preacher Wright said that he's going to pay him a huge amount of money. Jim Clanton is going to let him and his family continue to live there for six months after the sale. That way, Preacher Wright can find someone to take over his responsibilities down at the church before they have to move."

Charlie got up from the table to pour himself another cup of coffee and said, "Clanton has bought Turkey Holler Bill's place, and now he's going to buy Ken Martin's and Preacher Wright's places. There's not going to be too many families left on the mountain. Maybe I should sign over Lou's place to you, Dessie. Even though Lou's old shack ain't worth nothing, her 252 acres of land would bring a lot of money. Then you could sell your place and have enough money to move anywhere you want, maybe somewhere the winters aren't so cold."

"I'm not selling my and Hob's homeplace for no amount of money. I'll die on this old mountain," I said.

Charlie said, "Dessie, you sure are hardheaded. If everybody else sells out, you'll be stranded all alone on top of this mountain. It will be just you and Jim Clanton."

"You forgot about Mike Wall. Mike told me he's not selling his place," I said.

"Mike lives all the way at the foot of this mountain, and it takes him at least twenty minutes to drive up here. Who are you going to call if you need help right away?" Charlie asked.

Hattie said, "Charlie, Dessie can call me."

Charlie said, "You live four hundred miles away. It would take you at least five or six hours to drive all the way up here."

Hattie said, "Not if I move in with Dessie. I been thinking. I have nobody back in Georgia, and what family I have left is up here on Brushy Mountain. I been thinking about asking Dessie if I could rent the spare bedroom and come live with her."

"That's a wonderful idea. I would love for you to come live with me, except I won't charge you nothing," I said. "We can cook and raise a garden, and even though I know he don't mind, I won't have to bother Mike Wall for rides to town for groceries and such."

Hattie came over, gave me a huge hug, and said, "I'll go back to Georgia to gather my things after Lou's funeral. It shouldn't take me but a few days to return because I rent my home there. All I have to pack are the rest of my clothes and some keepsakes."

Charlie said he would feel a lot better if Hattie moved in with me. He said he had a moonshine still to run and couldn't be tied down. He added, "Besides, if Ken Martin and Preacher Wright leave, I don't care too much for the rest of the folks living on the mountain anyway."

The rest of the day wore on. Hattie and I had planned a catfish supper with all the trimmings. I went to the cellar and got some green beans, potatoes, and onions that I had stored from the garden last summer. Hattie prepared the fish by putting them in a bowl of buttermilk, then placing them in a paper bag filled with cornmeal, flour, salt, pepper, garlic salt, and just a touch of red pepper. While Hattie was working on the fish, I got a cookie sheet, cut the potatoes in half, and placed them skin sides down. I then took my knife and made several crisscross slits into the meat of the potatoes. Then I put lots of butter, salt, and pepper on top of each potato and placed them in the oven at four hundred degrees. Hattie made the hushpuppies using buttermilk, eggs, chopped green onions, and seasoning while I opened the can of green beans.

It wasn't long before Charlie, Hattie, and I had all we could possibly eat. Once we got onto the front porch, Charlie said that after Lou's funeral, he had to go make whiskey. His customers expected their shine at the same time every month, no matter what was happening. Charlie said that Mike would be staying with us until he got back. "I hope things around here get back to normal soon, so I can move back to my place on the New River," he added.

We all went to bed early that night, knowing we had a big day tomorrow with Lou's funeral. And I was sure to have a lot of friends stop by afterward.

By the time I got to the kitchen the next morning, Hattie already had a plate of bacon and flapjacks. After breakfast, I made a double batch of oatmeal cookies along with some teacakes, knowing we would need something to serve after the funeral.

It wasn't long until I heard the familiar sound of a truck stopping down by my mailbox. Hattie looked out the window and said, "Dessie, Mike Wall is here." Hattie and I were already dressed for the service, and Charlie had put on his best pair of overalls and a plaid flannel shirt.

When Charlie let Mike in, he said he would drive separately, so he could just head on over to his place and start making shine after Lou's funeral.

I said, "Charlie, you know we're going to have some people stop by after the service to pay their respects. If you're not here, how will that look?"

Charlie said, "If it's the same people that came by after Turkey Holler Bill's funeral, then I don't want to see them, especially that mean old ex-wife of mine, Dorothy. The only reason she comes is to aggravate me and eat your cookies and complain."

I couldn't help laughing and agreeing with my brother.

Mike parked in the same place he used at Turkey Holler Bill's funeral. He helped me and Hattie out of his truck and held on to my arm as we walked through the graveyard gates. I saw that Buford had done as he promised and prepared Lou's grave plot beside her sister Ida's. Standing around the big green tent covering Lou's plot were Dorothy, Mary Wright, Ken Martin and his wife, Shelby, April Brandon, Frail Jones, Michael Langford, and my two sons, Bill and Don. Also, there were several folks from Moravian Falls that I knew, including that sorry sheriff Bobby Spillman.

Lou's closed casket was covered in beautiful flowers, and more were placed around the gravesite. After the ceremony, Preacher Wright's wife, Mary, sang "Amazing Grace" as I walked to the casket and placed a yellow rose on top for Lou.

Mike held my arm when Hattie and I headed back to the truck. We were stopped short by Sheriff Bobby Spillman.

Sheriff Bobby said, "Dessie and Hattie, I am so sorry for your loss. I know how much you must have loved Lou. It's a tragedy that these things happen in life. Dessie, I plan on stopping by your place in a few days to make sure you're all right and safe. If you need anything before then, just give me a call."

I just smiled as I got into Mike's truck. I thought, *Maybe everything is going to be all right and get back to normal. Maybe they'll just leave me be.*

CHAPTER TWENTY-SIX

While we were still in the parking lot, Charlie walked over to Mike's truck and motioned for me to roll down the window. He asked, "What was that all about with the sheriff?"

I said, "The sheriff paid his respects to Hattie and me and said he'll check on us in a few days, and if we need anything, just to give him a call."

Charlie said, "That don't make any sense. Preacher Wright said that Jim Clanton was such a nice man, and we know how he threatened Hamp and even talked rough to you. Now the sheriff says he's concerned about you and Hattie. I don't trust that sorry Bobby Spillman. He ain't never been worth a hoot."

Mike spoke up and said, "Charlie, you go on and do what you have to do and don't worry about Dessie. I'll take real good care of Dessie and Hattie and make sure no harm comes their way."

Charlie said, "I should be back in a few days, Dessie. Make sure you save me some of them oatmeal cookies."

I turned to Mike and said, "We better get back home. I'm sure we'll have guests stop by to pay their respects."

When we rounded the final curve of that old road, I could

see a couple of trucks parked in front of my house and a few people sitting on my front porch. The first person to greet us was Dorothy, Charlie's ex-wife. She said, "Dessie, where have you been? I had to go in the house and put on a pot of coffee. I found the oatmeal cookies you baked for everyone on the kitchen table. I brought them onto the porch for your guests."

I said, "I'm sorry I wasn't back when you got here, Dorothy. I'm glad you made yourself at home."

Dorothy said, "Where is Charlie? He should be here helping you, Dessie. Lou was his cousin, too, you know."

"Charlie had to go to work but should be home in a few days. Do you want me to tell him you need to see him?" I asked.

"Heavens no. I just was wondering why he wasn't here with you and Hattie Mae," said Dorothy.

April Brandon and Michael Langford were sitting on the end of the porch in my old straight-back chairs enjoying a big glass of the sweet tea Hattie had made that morning. As I went over to greet them, I heard a truck coming up the road. When it rounded the final curve to my house, I saw that my sons, Bill and Don, had come to visit with our guests. In the back of Bill's truck were two long folding tables and several white plastic chairs. Mike Wall met my boys and helped set the tables and chairs under the poplar trees in the front yard. Don carried a fruit and vegetable tray, and Bill had a tray of chicken fingers and wings with all the sauces. Bill and Don greeted the folks as they put all the food on the folding tables.

More and more people began to arrive, until it almost seemed like the whole mountain was at my house. April Brandon brought deviled eggs and potato salad, and Mary Wright brought baked beans and coleslaw. Shelby Martin had a container filled with fried chicken and a big basket of her homemade yeast rolls. After placing their food on the table, each one of my friends and neighbors hugged me and Hattie and said how sorry they were that Lou was gone. When Mary Wright hugged me, she whispered, "We're going to miss you, Dessie. You made us feel welcome on this old Brushy Mountain, and we love you."

Soon, most of the food was gone, and I noticed all the men had moved their chairs away from the tables and were sitting in the shade of the poplar trees. Mike Wall, Bill, Don, Michael Langford, Preacher Wright, and Ken Martin were telling stories about Lou and Turkey Holler Bill. I went into the house to get the men a fresh pitcher of the sweet tea Hattie had made. When I returned to the group, I heard Bill say, "Don, tell us about the time Lou was in the hospital with pneumonia, and what happened when you went to visit her."

Don said, "Bill, don't nobody want to hear that stupid story. And besides, I'm trying to forget about it myself."

Bill said, "Okay, then I'll tell it."

Don said, "All right, Bill. If it has to be told, then I will tell it. At least that way, it will be the truth, and you won't be adding a bunch of lies to it."

All the menfolk moved their chairs closer to Don so they could make sure that got every word. Don said, "This happened about two years ago, when Uncle Charlie was making his monthly whiskey run to Lou's shack. Charlie found Lou and all her dogs lying on their bed. Lou looked in bad shape and was unresponsive when he called her name. He said that when he felt Lou's forehead, he could tell she was burning up with fever. Since Charlie couldn't get Lou to come around, he thought he better wrap her up and take her to the hospital.

"Charlie wrapped Lou up in an old blanket and put her in the cab of the truck, along with her favorite dog, Little Beaver. He then grabbed all of Lou's other dogs, put them in the back of his old truck, and headed down the mountain, going to the hospital. Charlie pulled that truck up to the emergency entrance like he owned the place. He left Lou in the truck, went into the hospital, and found an orderly pushing an empty stretcher. He yelled so everyone in the emergency room could hear that he had a dying woman in the cab of his truck. The orderly grabbed his stretcher and rushed to Charlie's truck. Charlie and the orderly gathered up Lou, put her on the stretcher, and rushed her into the hospital, where doctors were waiting on her. Once the doctors took Lou into the examining room, Charlie wrapped up Little Beaver, and the two of them waited in the lobby."

Don continued, "It wasn't long before an elderly doctor came into the lobby and told Charlie that Lou had double pneumonia but was stable. He said that Lou would have to stay in the hospital for a few days to take the necessary antibiotics, as well as breathing treatments.

"About four days later, I went to visit Lou to see how she was recovering and to make sure she didn't need anything. When I went into her room, I found Lou sitting in a lounge chair eating chicken noodle soup. She looked better than I had seen her in years and wanted me to stay with her and talk. About an hour later, a nurse came into the room and told me it was time for Lou to go on her walk around the nursing station to build up her lung capacity. I helped Lou up and held her arm as we walked three times around the nursing station and back into her room. Lou asked me to help her get back into bed and said that little walk had tuckered her completely out. Once she was in bed, I sat in the lounge chair beside her."

Don spoke a little louder to the group of men gathered around. "You know how when you get to eating cashews, it's almost impossible to stop? Well, a big bowl of cashews was sitting on the table beside Lou's bed, along with an unopened bottle of water. After about thirty minutes, I had eaten all of Lou's cashews. As I was saying my goodbyes, I told Lou how sorry I was that I had eaten all her nuts. Lou sat up in bed and said, 'Honey, don't you worry about that. I'm getting so old and my teeth are so bad that all I can do is just suck the chocolate off of them anymore.' "

CHAPTER TWENTY-SEVEN

The crowd started to dwindle as our neighbors and friends headed back down the mountain to their homes. Dorothy was the first to leave, since Charlie wasn't there for her to fuss at. But she made sure she gathered what food was left for her supper, and probably even breakfast the next morning.

Mike helped Don and Bill load the table and chairs while Hattie and I cleaned up the dishes and cups left by our guests. After Don and Bill headed down the mountain, Mike, Hattie, and I sat on the front porch and watched the day come to an end. We all turned in early, with Mike sleeping on the couch and Hattie in the guest bedroom.

As we were saying our good nights, Hattie said, "I want to get up early and head to my house in Georgia and gather up all my things." When she hugged me, she whispered, "Thank you for letting me come to live with you, Dessie. I should be back on the mountain within three days."

I got up early the next morning to find Mike stumbling around in the kitchen, looking for the canister of coffee. "Mike, let me make us a pot of coffee. What would you and Hattie like for breakfast?" I asked.

Mike said, "Hattie got up real early this morning and is

already on her way back to Georgia. She said she would pack up and be back here in a few days.”

“I hope Hattie will be safe. It worries me that she has that long drive by herself. I sure will be glad when she gets back home,” I said. “Mike, I’ll put us on a pot of grits, and we can scramble eggs for a good old country breakfast.”

Mike said that scrambled eggs and grits were his favorite breakfast but then added, “You’re going to make your famous biscuits, too, aren’t you, Dessie?”

After breakfast, I was beginning to clean up the kitchen when Mike asked, “Dessie, is there anything that needs fixing around the house? I’m a pretty good handyman, and I have my toolbox on the back of my truck. I feel like I need to earn my keep.”

“Mike, you just being here keeping me company until Charlie gets back is more than earning your keep,” I said. “But since you asked, at the toolshed out back are a couple of boards that have worked loose and need to be re-nailed.”

Mike said, “Great, Dessie. I’ll be out back working. But if you need me, just holler and I’ll be right here.”

I watched Mike go out the front door and down to his truck, where he gathered up an armful of tools and headed through the yard to my toolshed. After cleaning up the kitchen, I got a fresh cup of coffee and retired to my rocking chair on the front porch. While I was enjoying the day, I could hear Mike beating and banging around in the backyard, and I even heard an occasional cussword or two flying through the mountain air.

Around lunchtime, Mike took his tools back to his truck and came up on the porch. When he settled down in a rocking chair, I couldn't help noticing that his hat and shirt were soaking wet with sweat.

Mike asked, "Dessie, do you know what kind of wood that shed is built out of? I have never seen any wood like it. It's so hard that I had to drill starter holes in it before I could nail it back in place."

"My late husband, Hob, built that toolshed years ago from chestnut trees that we had growing on our property," I explained. "A blight came across all the mountains in North Carolina and killed every chestnut tree around. Hob cut down all our dead trees and with mules dragged them out of the woods. He and Ken Martin sawmilled them into rough-cut boards. Just about all the sheds and even some houses on this old mountain are built out of chestnut trees."

Mike said, "It's the hardest wood I've ever seen. If we had wood like that today, there wouldn't be no need for bricks."

We both laughed as I got up to fetch us a pitcher of sweet tea. When I got to the front door, I stopped and listened to the familiar sound of an approaching truck.

Mike said, "Dessie, you go on into the house until I see who's coming up the road."

I went into the living room and watched out the window as the sheriff's truck slowly came to a stop just behind Mike's. Sheriff Bobby Spillman and Jim Clanton got out and walked to the front porch.

Sheriff Bobby said, "Mike Wall, I didn't know you were here visiting Dessie. Me and Mr. Clanton have come by to check on her and Hattie to make sure they're all right."

I went to the kitchen and got the pitcher of tea and a tray of glasses. When I walked onto the front porch, I said, "Why, Sheriff Bobby Spillman and Mr. Clanton, y'all are just in time to enjoy a glass of sweet tea with Mike and me."

Jim Clanton spoke up and said, "You Southern hillbillies ruin tea by adding sugar. Real tea is served hot and in a cup like coffee, and not with ice, and certainly not with sugar."

I said, "You know, Mr. Clanton, I really don't like you very much."

Jim Clanton said, "Well, Dessie, most people don't."

With that, Mike stood up as if to say he had heard enough. The sheriff could tell there was tension on the porch. He said, "Now, Mike, let's not get angry. We just came by to check on

Dessie and Hattie. Where is Hattie? Her car isn't in the yard."

Before I could answer, Mike said, "Hattie went into town to run a few errands and will be returning shortly."

Jim Clanton butted in. "Look, Bobby. Enough with the small talk. Dessie, I've come up here to convince you to sell me your place, as well as Lou's." Then he added, "Mike, I'll buy your place as well. I'm really trying to be nice with y'all, as I was with Preacher Wright. I'm willing to pay top dollar for your land and even will let you stay in your home for up to six months after I buy it."

Mike looked straight at Jim Clanton and said, "My place ain't for sale, and there's no need in asking me about it anymore."

"I will never sell my home to you or anyone else. And as for Lou's place, she left it to Charlie when she died," I said. "So, Bobby, if y'all will kindly leave my property, Mike and I have a few more chores to do today."

As the two of them turned to walk away, I heard Mr. Clanton say, "See, Bobby? I told you that being nice wouldn't work with some of these hillbillies. I'll have to figure out a better way. Maybe we need to talk to old Charlie."

When Sheriff Bobby Spillman's truck was out of sight, Mike said, "We haven't seen the last of them two yet. Did you hear Jim Clanton say that maybe they need to talk to Charlie?"

"There ain't no need to talk to Charlie. He would never sell Lou's place to them or anybody else. If Charlie wants to get rid of Lou's place, he would give it to me. I wouldn't sell anything to that jackleg Jim Clanton," I said. "Mike, I'm going into the kitchen and start working on our supper. I think we'll be having pintos, fried catfish, fried potatoes, and onions, along with a big cake of cornbread."

Mike said, "I think I'll just piddle around out back here, check for loose boards, and explore some of the old tools you have in your shed."

After we ate supper and I cleaned up the kitchen, I told Mike that I was going to my bedroom. I said, "When I have worries on my mind, it does me good to read the Bible for comfort."

I must have dozed off, because I was startled when Mike tapped on my bedroom door. I went to the door and said, "Mike, what's wrong?"

Mike whispered, "Dessie, there's a man in the front yard. You stay in here, and I'll find out who he is and what he wants. Keep your door locked until I tell you everything is okay."

I looked at the old clock sitting on my nightstand, which showed that it was eleven-thirty. I thought, *Who would be standing in my yard this time of night, and for what reason?*

Not listening to Mike's advice, I put on my bathrobe and,

without cutting on any lights, made my way into the living room and looked through the window. In the full-moon light, I could see Mike approaching a man standing in the middle of my front yard. As Mike got closer, I could see that he had a pistol in his right hand and the stranger had a shotgun or rifle tucked under his right arm.

Then I heard Mike yell, "Frail Jones, what in the hell are you doing here?"

CHAPTER TWENTY-EIGHT

◆

After about ten minutes, Mike turned back toward the house and Frail walked through my front yard and crossed the dirt road. I opened the door and anxiously waited on Mike. As he walked onto the front porch, he said, "Nothing to worry about, Dessie. Frail was coon hunting down close to Mr. Martin's pond when he lost one of his old hounds. Frail thought that the dog might have come up the mountain to your house."

"What a relief! With all the crazy stuff going on around here, I thought we might be in trouble," I said.

"Nothing to worry about. I won't let nobody hurt you or Hattie Mae," said Mike. "Frail also wanted me to tell you and Hattie that he truly apologizes for the way he acted and the things he said at the sale of Turkey Holler Bill's place. He said he had been drinking a little white liquor throughout the day, and it must have gotten the best of him, and he is very sorry."

"Well, I'm glad he's gone, and I'll never trust him again, even if it was the liquor talking," I said. "I'll probably be up the rest of the night. My nerves are shot. I might as well make a pot of coffee to calm me down."

"Frail said that if an old bluetick hound comes around, he'd be much obliged if we would tie him up and give him a call," said Mike. "Funny, though, Frail asked me at least twice where Charlie and his old truck were, and he also asked about Hattie. I told him that Charlie was at work and Hattie was visiting friends back in Georgia, and that I would be here with you until they both return."

The next morning, I was startled awake by the sound of banging pots and pans coming from the kitchen. Mike had already fried sausage and eggs for breakfast and was trying to clean up the dishes.

"Good morning, Dessie," Mike said. "I just finished cooking me some breakfast, and as soon as I wash this frying pan, I'll be more than happy to fix you some sausage and eggs, if you want."

"That's sweet of you to ask, but I think I'll just have a couple of oatmeal cookies and a strong cup of black coffee for breakfast," I said. "My nerves are still shot from last night and Frail scaring me half to death."

Just as I finished pouring my first cup of coffee, the telephone rang from the living room. Mike said, "I'll get it. You finish your coffee and cookies."

After a short time, Mike came back into the kitchen and said, "It was Hattie Mae on the phone. She said she'll be home today around two o'clock. She said that her landlord came over and helped her pack all her things, and that she's on her way home.

She sounded excited and can hardly wait to get here."

"Mike, why don't you go sit in the sunshine on the porch with your coffee while I finish cleaning up the kitchen," I said. "I also want to change the sheets on Hattie's bed and straighten up her room to make it all cozy for her when she gets home. Now all we need is for Charlie to come back, and maybe our little family and this old mountain can get back to normal."

After a few cookies and a quick cup of coffee, I went to work straightening up Hattie's room and the rest of my small home. Before I knew it, the whole house was clean and it was almost lunchtime. I thought, *I'll open a can of soup and fix Mike and me a sandwich for lunch while we wait on Hattie to get home.*

It was about twelve-thirty when I called Mike in from the porch for lunch. While we were eating, we heard the familiar sound of a truck driving up the old mountain road.

Mike said, "Wow! Hattie must have made really good time. She said she wouldn't be here until about two."

Mike and I got up from the kitchen table and headed straight for the front porch to greet Hattie Mae. When we got there, I was shocked to see Sheriff Bobby Spillman's truck parked by the mailbox. "Darn, I was hoping that she had gotten home early," I said. "Instead of seeing my beautiful Hattie Mae, I get that jackleg sheriff Bobby Spillman. I wonder what he wants."

We watched as the sheriff got out of his truck, adjusted his hat and gun belt, and walked straight to Mike and me. When he got close to the front porch, he took off his hat and said, "Dessie, you should probably sit down. I have terrible news to tell you."

My knees buckled as Mike helped me to my rocking chair. I was wondering what sad news this man was about to tell me. Thoughts raced through my mind that something terrible must have happened to Hattie Mae on her way home. Sitting in my rocking chair, I looked up at Sheriff Bobby Spillman, waiting on his terrible news.

Sheriff Bobby put his hand on mine and said, "Dessie, Charlie's dead."

I burst out in tears as Mike came over to comfort me. "Please, Lord, not my Charlie!" I screamed.

"Some boys fishing down by the New River found Charlie's truck stranded in the middle of the river," said Bobby Spillman. "When they opened the truck and found Charlie's body, they hightailed it out of there and came and got me. When I got down and opened the truck, I found that Charlie had been shot in the chest with what appeared to be a shotgun. I figured that someone who knew Charlie and where his moonshine still was tried to rob him, and it turned out bad. Charlie's still was scattered about, and his place was ransacked by whoever killed him. Dessie, I'll find out who did this, and I promise you I will make them pay."

I just looked up at the sheriff and thought, *Who would want to kill Charlie? He probably didn't have more than a hundred dollars to his name. His moonshine still was probably worth more than any amount of cash he had, but they didn't take the still. Don't make no sense.*

I then stood up and said, "Mike, will you please help me back into the house? I feel that I'm going to be sick."

Sheriff Bobby Spillman said, "I'll keep y'all posted and will let you know when we have any leads or suspects."

While Mike was helping me to my bedroom, I heard the sound of another car approaching and turned just in time to see Hattie Mae coming up our old dirt road.

CHAPTER TWENTY-NINE

The next day was just a blur. Mike and Hattie greeted relatives and friends that came to pay their respects. I stayed in my bedroom, thinking about poor old Charlie and who would want to kill such a kind man. Charlie would give you the shirt off his very back if he thought you needed it. I cried off and on most all of the day. Hattie brought me coffee and some food that our friends dropped at the house.

Later that afternoon after all our guests left, I managed to get dressed and went and sat on the front porch.

Mike came onto the porch, sat in the rocker beside me, took my hand in his, and said, "Dessie, I know you're hurting, but Charlie wouldn't want you to grieve yourself to death. Don't worry. I'll stay with you and Hattie until the killer is found and things get back to normal."

"Mike, did you know that Charlie and me grew up on this old mountain?" I asked. "We had a small home down off Brock Town Road close to where you built your house. My daddy made moonshine and worked in the apple orchards, and in the summertime, he traveled to West Virginia and worked in the coal mines. Dad always seemed to get enough money to pay for the necessities. At Christmas, Dad would take Charlie and cut down a small cedar tree. Mama and I would decorate it with pine cones and holly berries. If we had enough money, Mama would buy popcorn down in Moravian, and we'd string it together with sewing thread, making garland for our Christmas tree. Every Christmas morning, Charlie and I got a big paper sack of candy, apples, oranges, pears, and hard-shell nuts from Santa."

Hattie came onto the porch, handed me a fresh cup of coffee, and sat in the rocker beside Mike.

Mike said, "Dessie, sounds like you and Charlie had a great childhood."

"We played in all the creeks and streams around and explored every inch of this old mountain," I said. "In the summertime, Charlie and I would leave the house right after all our chores were done and stay out all day until dusk. Mama would make us pies from all the blueberries, blackberries, and hickory nuts that we gathered. Mike, have you ever ate a hickory nut pie?"

Mike said, "Can't say that I have, Dessie."

"Well, it's a lot like pecan pie, except a whole lot better," I said. "It takes a lot of hickory nuts to make just one pie."

I told Hattie and Mike what happened one day when Charlie and I were out exploring. We spotted a hawk's nest high in the top of a tall pine tree. Charlie said, "Dessie, you stay down here while I climb up to the nest and see if there are baby hawks in it. I always wanted a hawk to train to help me catch squirrels and rabbits and such. Just think how proud Dad will be if me and my hawk can catch enough meat for us for the entire winter."

Charlie wouldn't listen to reason. In a flash, up the tree he went. I watched as he got closer and closer to the hawk's nest. Finally, Charlie looked into the nest and hollered, "There are five good-size baby hawks in here! I'm going to put one in each of my coat pockets and head back down." Charlie was so excited.

Just then, I saw a huge mama hawk screaming and flying through the trees, headed in Charlie's direction. Before I could yell and alarm him, the huge white and brown hawk flew hard into the side of Charlie's face, knocking him loose from his perch. Charlie fell out of the tree, breaking branches as he dropped. All the while, the mother hawk was chasing and flogging him on his way down. Finally, with a big thump, Charlie hit the ground with the hawk still on his back. He jumped up and grabbed one of the broken pine limbs to protect himself, but he and I both realized immediately that he had fallen into a yellow jacket nest. The two of us ran through the woods as fast as we could with the mama hawk flogging us all the way while yellow jackets were stinging every exposed part of our bodies.

When we finally got home, our eyes were just about swollen

shut from all the bee stings. Hearing our screams, Mama came running from the house to see who or what was killing us. When she finally realized that Charlie had fallen from a tall pine and that both of us were eat up with yellow jacket stings, she grabbed us up and rushed into the house. Once inside, Mama started doctoring us by making a paste out of baking soda and vinegar and putting a big glob on each of our stings.

After several hours, when she saw that we would live, Mama made Charlie go out and fetch a switch from an apple tree. After a big whooping from the apple switch, Mama said, "That's what you two get for being so dumb as to try to rob a hawk's nest. Mamas will fight to the death to protect their babies, both animals and humans, and don't y'all two ever forget that."

Hattie laughed and said, "It's funny now, but I bet it wasn't funny then."

I simply smiled and said, "I still have nightmares about all those yellow jackets and their stings. I'm scared to death of them even to this day."

It wasn't long until the sun went down and the night sounds of crickets and tree frogs serenaded the whole mountain. The wind began to pick up, and we

could hear the comforting sounds of poplar leaves blowing onto the old tin roof.

Hattie said, "Dessie, I want to thank you for letting me come live with you, and I hope you know how much I love you. Now that Charlie is gone, you and I will just have to take care of each other. I promise everything is going to be all right."

When I lay down on my bed, I couldn't help thinking about Charlie and how scared he must have been right before he was shot. My mind was racing, thinking about who could have been so mean as to shoot such a good man.

Just after daylight, I was awakened by the sound of an old hound dog wailing as if it had just treed a coon in my front yard. I got dressed and went to the kitchen to find Hattie making coffee and Mike putting on his jacket.

Mike said, "By the sound of things, I guess Frail Jones has found his bluetick hound. I'll go out and see if he needs any help and try to get him to hush his old dog."

I heard Mike yell, "Frail, is that you?" as he stood on the front porch. I jumped when the sound of a shotgun exploding seemed to shake the whole house. The blast from the gun knocked Mike against the front door. I looked through the window and plainly saw Billy Barr standing in the yard, pointing a shotgun toward Mike. Just then, I heard the siren of Sheriff Bobby Spillman's truck screaming up our old dirt road. I watched as the sheriff slid to a stop at my mailbox. With his gun drawn, Sheriff Bobby jumped out of the truck and ran through the yard toward Billy Barr. Sheriff Bobby demanded that Billy drop his gun. Then I watched as Jim Clanton opened the passenger door and walked slowly and calmly toward the sheriff and Billy Barr.

Billy Barr yelled, "Jim, tell your boy to get that pistol out of my face and calm down!"

In amazement, I heard Jim yell to Sheriff Bobby to calm down and put his gun up. He said, "Bobby, Billy works for me, and he and I planned to meet here this morning."

Sheriff Bobby turned toward Jim Clanton and demanded, "What do you mean he works for you? He just shot Mike Wall."

Billy said, "Yeah, I just shot Mike. And I killed Turkey Holler Bill, Lou, and Charlie, and they ain't never going to find Hamp's body. I bet that this old bluetick hound won't be able to find where I buried Frail Jones either."

Sheriff Bobby said, "Wait a minute, Jim. I agreed to strong-arm these mountain folks so they would sell their land to you, but I didn't sign on to anything having to do with murder."

Jim Clanton looked at the sheriff and said, "Bobby, are you really that dumb? You had to know Turkey Holler Bill was beat to death, and that there was no way old lady Lou could shoot herself with her own shotgun. If Charlie was killed by a liquor sale gone bad, don't you think they would have taken his moonshine still and equipment? Are you really that stupid? Well, Bobby, you're in it up to your eyeballs, so you might as well see this thing through."

Billy spoke up. "Now it's time for me to get paid, Jim, just like we agreed. Ida, Lou, Hamp, Charlie, Frail, and Mike at a thousand apiece. I figure you owe me six thousand dollars."

Jim said, "The deal isn't quite finished, Billy. Mike is not yet dead. I hear him moaning. And what about Dessie and Hattie? Where are their bodies?"

"Mike will bleed to death," said Billy. "Dessie and Hattie are inside the house, and if you want them dead, you'll have to do it yourself. I won't hurt Dessie. Her husband, Hob, was the only friend I had on this entire mountain, and there is no way I'm killing her or Hattie."

Hattie looked scared to death when I locked her in her bedroom and told her not to come out, no matter what.

I slowly and quietly went into my bedroom and got my old shotgun, knowing that I was going to have to shoot the first person that tried to come in the front door. I made my way back to the door and watched the three men shouting at each other in my front yard.

"Jim, it's time for me to get paid. You or Bobby will have to do the rest of the killing yourself," said Billy.

I watched as Jim reached into his coat pocket and pulled out what appeared to be a big envelope stuffed with money. He walked toward Billy holding out the envelope with his left hand and said, "Here's your money, Billy."

When Jim Clanton handed Billy the envelope, he reached into his right pocket and pulled out a small pistol. I watched as the gun exploded, shooting Billy square between the eyes.

Both Sheriff Bobby and I screamed at the sight of Billy's head being split open from the blast. He fell right where he was standing, and I could see the fear in the sheriff's eyes, thinking he might be next.

I watched Jim Clanton slowly turn toward Bobby and heard him say, "You're going to have to clean this mess up while I take care of Dessie and Hattie."

Just as I was thinking that I would have to shoot Jim Clanton, I heard what sounded like a dozen sirens blasting up the mountain. I stood at my front door as six trucks slid to a stop in the middle of the road just behind Sheriff Bobby's truck. On the side of each was painted FBI in big, bold, black letters. I counted twenty-four agents jumping from the trucks with their weapons drawn. Most had rifles or pistols, and each one was pointed toward Bobby Spillman and Jim Clanton. Soon, Sheriff Bobby and Jim Clanton were handcuffed and placed in the backseat of separate FBI trucks.

I watched as the most elderly agent made his way to attend to Mike on the front porch. I opened the door, and the agent said to me, "He's going to be just fine. The shot hit him in the top of his right shoulder, and an ambulance is on its way." Then the agent stood up, shook my hand, and said, "My name is Lane Parrish. Your brother, Charlie, was my best friend." Lane told me how sorry he was to hear that Charlie had been killed. He said that he and Charlie went to school together and fished and hunted together while growing up on this old mountain. Lane said, "I've been retired from the Bureau for some time now—that is, until I got a call from Charlie and Hattie's friend, FBI agent James Parker. After James's phone call, I found out that the Bureau had been investigating the sheriff for a long time, and that they added Jim Clanton to the investigation a few weeks ago."

Lane handed me his card and said that if Hattie or I ever needed anything, he was just a phone call away.

Soon after the ambulance left with Mike and the medical examiner did his duty with Billy Barr, Lane and all the other agents headed down the road and back into their world.

Then it was just Hattie and me all alone in my old house, trying to calm our nerves and reflecting on what just happened. It was quiet except for a gentle breeze blowing through the poplar trees when we were both startled by a scratching sound coming from our front door. With my shotgun in hand, I slowly opened the door to find Little Beaver sitting on my porch, wagging his tail as if to say, *I'm finally home.*

"Well, Mary, now you know the whole story about the Brushy Mountain killings, and I hope your boss will be happy with your work."

Mary said, "Miss Dessie, how can I tell you how grateful I am? The killing of your family and friends on this mountain is something I will never forget, no matter what my boss or readers say. I hope that after the story is printed, you'll allow me to bring supper for you and Hattie as my way of thanking you."

When Hattie, Mary, and I said our final goodbyes, I opened the front door, and there sat Little Beaver on the porch, wagging his tail as if to say, Don't forget about me.

THE END

KILLER

JACK SNOW

PROLOGUE

Few people come to visit anymore. Oh, occasionally, a lost carful of kids looking for the amusement park and sometimes one of my daughters or grandchildren will stop by for a short visit. But Bonnie and I do just fine living off the side of this old mountain overlooking Blowing Rock, North Carolina. Now in our early seventies, we have resigned ourselves to a simpler life and a simpler existence. I haven't hunted since the tragedy, and I don't even have the desire to wet a fishing hook. Bonnie and I just want to live the remainder of our days left alone. Lots of nights, we find ourselves quietly rocking on this old front porch, listening to the mountains. I never knew that mountains could communicate with one's soul, but this old Blue Ridge mountain has done wonders to help me forget. Many nights, I get lost in the mountain's winds, letting them carry me back to our old home, to a better time when our friends were close and our family even closer.

But not this particular day because we had a visitor who brought back all the bad memories Bonnie and I thought we had left back in Davie County. This morning, just after a country breakfast, I got up from the table as usual and emptied the scraps of country ham, eggs, and grits from my plate back into the skillet. I knew that my old bird dog, Sadie, was ready to eat her morning's due. Sadie, her hunting spirit broken like mine, was now retired and resigned to living the rest of her days in whatever peace came her way. As I opened the screen door on the back porch, headed for Sadie's dog pen, I heard the familiar sound of a lost car slowly approaching this old cabin. Our gravel road has a sound of its own. The rocks disheveled by the automobile gave me a sense of neither fright nor calm, but one of anticipation of who was disturbing my world, and for what reason. As the new, shiny car rolled to a stop, I strolled from the backyard around to the front porch to greet this lost tourist.

Just as I reached the front yard, the car door slowly opened, and a pudgy, overweight young man emerged. The first things I noticed, other than his size, were a flashy earring and baggy, drooping jeans. *Another lost kid looking for the amusement park has gotten off the main highway and onto my long dirt driveway and right into my world*, I thought.

"Go back the way you came. It's two miles to the hard-surface road. Take a left, then go exactly 2.8 miles and turn left on Highway 421. The amusement park is on the right," I said.

The young man looked deep into my eyes and asked, "Is your name Rumsey, Jack Rumsey?"

A sense of fear, almost a sickening feeling, ran through my body, and I was just barely able to get the words out. "Who wants to know?" I said.

"My name is Cannon Swain, and I live in Mocksville," he softly said. After a few seconds of silence, he added, "And if you're Jack Rumsey, I've been looking for you for over a year now."

Turning my back to him, I said more forcibly, "Yeah, I'm Jack Rumsey, and I don't know any Swains, so kindly turn your damn car around and leave me be."

"My grandpa was Yeoman Swain, and I need you to help me understand about him," he said.

My body froze, just like when, as a kid, I jumped into the creek after getting up hay all day in August. To keep from falling down, I stepped onto the front porch to sit and take a closer look at this young man. "That was years ago, a time I have forgotten and do not wish to remember, so just get back in your car and leave me be," I said.

The young man just stared into my eyes once more and quietly said, "May I just sit with you awhile?"

My mind, body, and soul wanted to say no, but to my horror I simply waved for him to sit in Bonnie's rocking chair.

This young man was all of only five-foot-two and must have weighed at least 275 pounds. He had sandy brown hair, blue eyes, a baby face, and a real white complexion and was the spitting image of a young friend long forgotten. When Cannon began to step onto the porch, his big foot slipped on the old granite rock used for a step, and he must have fallen for what seemed like minutes. When he finally landed, I couldn't help laughing out loud at the sight, just as I would have if it had been my old friend Yeoman himself.

As I jumped from my rocking chair to help him up, Bonnie came through the house, opened the screen door, and hollered, "What's going on? Who are you, and what are you doing here?"

"Bonnie," I said, "this clumsy young man is Cannon Swain, and he just stopped by to talk."

"Well, you can talk all you want, but we are not buying anything, and besides, you don't need to be wasting time talking. You and I both have a garden to tend to," she snapped.

I looked over at Bonnie as I finished helping Cannon to her chair. "This is Yeoman Swain's grandson," I explained. Excited fear flashed in my wife's eyes as she grabbed my arm in concern. I pulled her close to me and said reassuringly, "It's okay, dear. Let's just listen to what he has to say, and then we'll send him on his way. If he's anything like Yeoman, now that he's found us, if we don't listen, he'll just keep coming back and bothering us."

"Well, he's not sitting in my rocking chair. As young as he is, let him sit in the straight-back chair," Bonnie said, trying to sound more courageous.

As Bonnie and I sat in our rocking chairs, a warm, gentle spring breeze rustled through the leaves of the poplar trees almost on cue to calm our nerves. We didn't know what this young man had to say, or what information he wanted, but for some reason we just knew he meant us no harm.

I detected a quiver in his chubby chin and his voice as he began to speak. "My name is Cannon Swain, and I live by myself in Mocksville. My parents died in a car crash when I was eight, and I was sent to live with foster parents until I graduated from high school, just a little over two years ago. When I graduated, not having any family, and with nowhere to go, it was an easy decision for me to try to join the army. That's why I'm here."

"Wait a minute, son. I can't help you get into the army. I don't have any connections there or even know anyone in the army," I tried to explain.

"No, no, you don't understand. I'm not here for that. I'm here to learn about my grandfather," he softly said. "You see, when I went for my physical to get into the army, they found that, well, I'm dying. I have untreatable cancer and have only approximately nine months to live."

What do you say when someone, especially someone you don't know, tells you he's dying? I slowly rose to my feet and walked over to the young man. "I'm sorry to hear your sad news, but I don't see how I can help. So, if you'll excuse me, my wife and I have to work in the garden," I said, looking into his troubled eyes.

"I just want to know what really happened to my grandpa before I die. I've asked all over the county and spoken to everyone I can find who knew my grandpa, about his death. The answer I always get is that only Jack Rumsey knows what really happened to Yeoman. That's exactly why I'm here," he calmly said.

Nothing but silence was left among the three of us on the porch. Bonnie and I now knew why this young stranger had tracked me down.

Bonnie was the first to move. Rising from her rocking chair, she slowly strolled by and bent to whisper in my ear, "You owe this man an answer."

I whispered back, "I owe this man nothing. I'm sorry for his illness, but I owe him nothing. I'm just trying to forget."

Bonnie then smiled, gently held my hand in hers, looked at the sick young man, and said aloud, "Then you owe it to your close friend Yeoman." She then turned, opened the screen door, and retired into the old log house.

The two of us must have sat there on the porch for only a few minutes, but it seemed like hours. My mind flashed back to happier times, when Bonnie and I lived on our small farm and I used to hunt, fish, and sit around campfires with Yeoman and other friends. We would sit for hours eating, drinking, and telling hunting and fishing lies. During those simple times, my friends and I had developed bonds and lasting friendships that I thought even death would not destroy.

Not realizing my head was bowed, I slowly raised my tear-filled eyes to find this young man staring at me, waiting for an answer.

I barely whispered, "If I tell you the real story of your grandfather, will you then go and leave me in peace?"

He simply nodded.

"Well, Cannon, where do I start? Guess I'll just start from the time in Davie County when Bonnie and I were the happiest."

Chapter One

It was a cool, brisk November day, and the leaves were flying off the trees by the thousands. Half asleep sitting in my easy chair just under the front porch of my new garage, I was fully awakened when a damp, cold, wet rag hit me directly in the face.

"Thought you were cooking hamburgers for your hunting buddies today," my wife said, giggling about the wet rag. Bonnie and I had been married for thirty-three years then, and I've said many times that if God actually put angels on this earth, I was lucky enough to marry one. She was a beautiful woman who had not been damaged by the years or the tough times we endured making a living or the pleasures of raising three lovely daughters.

"I'm getting up," I said. "Besides, I've got plenty of time."

"No, you don't. You haven't even swept your hunting garage," Bonnie said.

I had always wanted a combination garage and hunting, fishing, and party shed, and in April, on my fifty-second birthday, Bonnie had hired my friend Larry Wyatt to build my dream. "The Shed," the likes of which no sportsman in Davie County, North Carolina, had ever seen, was absolutely the perfect hangout for me and my hunting buddies. The Shed was thirty by thirty-six feet and two stories, with a huge front porch, lots of ceiling fans, inside cedar paneling, a manly bathroom, a gun safe, a refrigerator full of beer, concrete stained floors, a full kitchen, a wood heating stove, and lots and lots of tools. I even had tools to fix other tools in my perfect, man's dream hunting and party shed.

"Screw the cleaning. The guys only care about beer, food, and telling stories. We're probably going to eat outside anyway," I added, trying to keep from doing any work.

"Suit yourself. I could care less about your mesquite

pit-cooked hamburgers and your hunting lies anyway," Bonnie said.

"Then shut up and get yourself back in the house, but give me a kiss before you leave," I said. She and I both knew I was just kidding about the shutting up part, but I was serious about the kiss. It was just my luck she turned and went strolling across the yard and into the house.

I had invited the local hunting guys over for hamburgers cooked over a fire pit of mesquite wood. In North Carolina, mesquite wood cooking is a delightful experience. Mesquite is a small bush or tree almost black in color, found mostly in southwest Texas. This wood burns extremely hot and creates an aroma and flavor all its own. In fact, mesquite wood chips sold in local stores are very expensive. This particular mesquite wood was shipped to me by my friend Blaine Thomas. Blaine was born and raised in Laredo, Texas, a cow town about thirty miles north of Mexico. Blaine had gotten out of the cow business and was now in the hunting and fishing business. During hunting season, he made a good living leasing ranches and selling south Texas deer hunts to people just like me. In the off-season, he guided saltwater pit-cooked hamburgers and your hunting lies anyway," Bonnie said.

"Then shut up and get yourself back in the house, but give me a kiss before you leave," I said. She and I both knew I was just kidding about the shutting up part, but I was serious about the kiss. It was just my luck she turned and went strolling across the yard and into the house.

I had invited the local hunting guys over for hamburgers cooked over a fire pit of mesquite wood. In North Carolina, mesquite wood cooking is a delightful experience. Mesquite is a small bush or tree almost black in color, found mostly in southwest Texas. This wood burns extremely hot and creates an aroma and flavor all its own. In fact, mesquite wood chips sold in local stores are very expensive. This particular mesquite wood was shipped to me by my friend Blaine Thomas. Blaine was born and raised in Laredo, Texas, a cow town about thirty miles north of Mexico. Blaine had gotten out of the cow business and was now in the hunting and fishing business. During hunting season, he made a good living leasing ranches and selling south Texas deer hunts to people just like me. In the off-season, he guided saltwater trout-fishing excursions in the Baytown area. Blaine was a good guy, a good friend, and a halfway decent guide.

Slowly but surely, the guys began to show up, looking for cold beer and something to snack on while the burgers cooked and the hunting lies flew. First to arrive was Larry Wyatt, a local builder well known and respected throughout the county. The most famous work of Larry's was The Shed, or at least the most famous to me. Larry was a tall, lanky man who laughed more than he talked and had never met a stranger. Larry was respected by his peers as a good sportsman and avid deer hunter. Next to arrive were my two next-door neighbors, Delmar Haines and Buford Wilson. Delmar and Buford were also the best of friends, even though Buford was Delmar's brother-in-law. Both were avid deer hunters. Neither Delmar, Buford, nor Larry were good wing shooters or cared much about any other type of hunting or fishing. JP, Delmar Haines's son, was the next to arrive. JP, a big country boy with a six-pack appreciation, came riding up to The Shed on his new 650 Arctic Cat ATV.

"Can't ride this and dip Copenhagen, too," mumbled JP through a half-hardy grin.

"Why not?" asked Buford.

"Goes so fast, spits the shit in my eyes," JP answered.

JP was the only man I knew below thirty-five years old who had a short flat-top haircut. I probably would not call JP a Davie County redneck, but he was as close to it as I guess I was. He and I had begun hunting and fishing together about six years earlier. In that time, I watched JP mature into a fine young man. He was honest, hardworking, and above all a loyal friend.

We were all standing around the fire pit and admiring JP's new ATV when Buford asked, "Where's Mike and Brian?"

Before anyone could answer, Delmar added, "And Yeoman. I've never known Yeoman to miss any meals."

"I'll have you know, I've lost fifty pounds on the Atkins Diet," Yeoman yelled from The Shed. "All I eat is dadgum chicken, though. Every meal, chicken, chicken, chicken. Why, I've ate so much chicken, I wake up in the mornings with the taste of wet feathers in my mouth."

Everyone around the pit roared with laughter.

Yeoman was as well known throughout the county as any man. You just couldn't help liking Yeoman. He weighed close to 350 pounds, was about five-foot-four, and always had a dip of tobacco in his mouth and a smile on his face. He was almost like a modern-day Santa Claus with his kindness for people, especially children. He knew everyone in Davie, their mothers and fathers, and probably a story about their families. I suspected that many of the stories Yeoman told, if not all of them, stretched the truth a lot, but no one in our hunting group ever got tired of hearing them.

I first met Yeoman many years ago. I was new to Davie County, and just on a whim I decided to run for county commissioner. Yeoman was campaign manager for his longtime friend Layne Watson. Layne, like Yeoman, was well known throughout the county. Layne was campaigning for commissioner because of his love for the land, its country nature, and the people who lived and worked there every day. Yeoman did a great job as campaign manager, and he and his candidate beat me by a landslide. My total campaign was giving out pens, cups, and chewing tobacco at Andy's Country Store. Andy's was where all the local farmers and just good old country boys hung out drinking Cokes, telling lies, chewing tobacco, and huddling around the wood stove.

These things passed the time for a lot of my friends. When everyone gathered around the wood stove, I would seize the opportunity to ask for their votes for commissioner.

One day while I was trying to drum up a few votes, Yeoman cut my speech short by interrupting. "You don't stand a chance, young man." Yeoman made sure he spoke loud enough for the entire crowd of Coke drinkers to hear. "We don't know you, and us folks around this county don't cotton to outsiders trying to come here and run things."

It was true that my wife and I had recently bought forty-three acres in Davie when we moved from neighboring Forsyth County.

"It's true you and Layne will probably beat me like a borrowed mule, but I'll still be in the hunt. Yeoman, I know I'll get at least four votes come Election Day," I said, waiting for him to fall into the trap I had just laid.

Yeoman took off his sweat-rimmed ball cap and said, "Wait a darn minute. You and your wife and three daughters can vote. To my count, that adds up to five."

"Don't think my youngest daughter, Kathy, is going to vote for me," I answered.

Everyone around the wood stove either roared with laughter or was trying to laugh but was choking on Coke and chewing tobacco.

Every day, Yeoman and I replayed this routine. And every day, I would answer the same. Yeoman would wheeze with laughter, slap me on the back, and say, "For someone from Forsyth County, Rumsey, you're all right, but we'll still whip you on Election Day."

Election Day came and went, and they did beat me, but I really was the winner because I had a new great friend in Yeoman Swain.

Yeoman liked to hunt almost as much as anyone in our group. He hunted deer, turkeys, doves, rabbits, squirrels, and any other animals that were legal to shoot.

Delmar grabbed the shovel and began to spread the hot mesquite coals in the fire pit. "This fire looks ready to me," he said.

 Buford said, "Then reckon I ought to get the grill top so we can get this party started."

Buford and I walked down to the pole barn, where the grill top hung from a sixteen-penny nail driven into the main beam of the barn. The pole barn was twenty feet deep and thirty feet wide, with an open front and six-inch boards down both sides and the back. The poles that supported the barn and the roof were made of treated six-by-six-inch lumber, braced by treated two-by-four-inch crossbars. The roof was red metal attached by one-inch screws placed about every two feet across each section. Buford and Delmar, along with me, JP, and Don and Matt Markland, helped build this barn just before deer season. We built it approximately a hundred yards from The Shed, and I used it to store a Kubota tractor, an Arctic Cat ATV, a Turf Tiger commercial lawn mower, and lawn mower attachments. One thing was for sure—that pole barn would be standing long after I was gone.

"The old barn looks good, even though you and Delmar built it," said Buford.

"What do you mean, me and Delmar? You and Delmar were the ones that really built this thing. JP, Don, Matt, and I just carried boards and beer to you two. I can't build nothing, fix nothing, or paint nothing. Thank goodness God gave me a mouth, because if I couldn't sell, me and Bonnie would starve to death," I said.

"You're right. You are the best salesperson I've ever met. I bet you could sell used underwear back to Hanes. Me, I couldn't sell a whore in a lumber camp, so I have to be good with my hands. Hard work is my life," Buford explained with a grin on his face.

"Are you going to grab the other side of this grill, or are we going to stay down here and jaw all night?" I asked.

As we carried the grill top back to the pit, it was evident that Mike and Brian had arrived. Brian had already jumped on JP's new ATV and was cutting donuts in the pasture beside The Shed.

"He's going to kill himself one of these days," Buford said.

When he was a kid, Brian used to race dirt bikes all around the county. He had broken about every bone in his body, and his shoulder blade at least three times. I don't guess he ever figured out that maybe he was just not built to ride those things. Brian had to be pushing seven feet tall. He was long and lanky and thin as a rail. Brian was Larry Wyatt's youngest son and had exactly the same personality as Larry. Brian, who had recently married, lived about two miles from me and had a real nice piece of land with a single-wide mobile home. He was a true Davie County redneck who once got struck by lightning while holding on to a CB antenna. All this boy knew was work. Right out of high school, Brian went to work grading and hauling for the local builders. He once told me that besides hunting and fishing, work was his favorite pastime. I had hunted and fished with Brian for many years and found him to be a real sportsman. He was always ready to hunt and did so with the passion and zeal of a fourteen-year-old kid. Brian loved hunting all kinds of game, including quail and ducks, but deer hunting was his passion.

I saw that Mike had found the washtub filled with beer and ice and had already cracked the top on one and was looking for the pre-dinner snacks.

"Where are your famous Redneck Caviar and chips?" Mike asked.

"In the refrigerator!" I yelled as Buford and I placed the grill on the pit of hot mesquite coals. Everyone loved my Redneck Caviar.

"What's in that stuff, anyway?" Buford asked.

"Well, it's simple. You just combine two cans of black-eyed peas, two cans of shoepeg corn, two cans of Rotel tomatoes, one green pepper, diced, one red pepper, diced, a dozen small green onions, chopped, and a bottle of Italian dressing. Chill for one hour and serve with tortilla chips," I replied. It was a great recipe that hit the spot with hunters, buddies, and fellow beer drinkers.

I lost sight of Mike when he headed for the refrigerator, followed very closely by Yeoman. I'd known Mike Dillion since I was just three years old. His uncle Charles was the meanest and roughest man in Forsyth County, and was married to my aunt on my mother's side. So he and I kind of grew up together, went to school together, played football and baseball together, but most of all hunted and fished together. Mike was just a couple of years older than I, and we had about the same build and weight. He was about five-foot-nine and weighed about 175 pounds. He had black hair and a friendly personality. Several years ago, Mike bought a farm just down the road from my place. His farm was absolutely beautiful. It had approximately eighty-two acres, with a real nice brick home overlooking a five-acre lake. His lake had tons of three-to ten-pound bass and plenty of channel catfish and bream. Many nights, Mike, JP, and I fished, drank beer, and fried catfish until the wee hours of the morning.

Yeoman was the first to break the silence after Buford and I positioned the grill top just right over the coals. "When are we going to eat?" he asked.

"Is that all you think about, Yeoman? 'Sides, you've got a big bowl of Redneck Caviar and chips," Delmar joked.

Before Yeoman could answer, Brian slid the Arctic Cat to a stop, jumped off, and said, "Yeoman, I thought you and Dr. Atkins were on a diet."

Yeoman looked puzzled about whom to answer first, and just simply looked at me and said, "Are you going to cook burgers or not?" He then turned to Brian and Delmar and said, "Look, let's get off the diet stuff, okay? I used to have to pull my britches down just to put my hands in my pockets, but now with Dr. Atkins's help, I can do that standing or sitting, thank you very much."

JP interrupted as he came from the kitchen of The Shed, headed toward the fire pit with a huge tray of burgers that appeared to be about a pound apiece. "Get out of the way,

Yo-Man. These burgers are heavy," JP announced in an annoying voice.

"Man, these are going to be good. One cup of water per pound of burger, and with all the seasonings I added, these will melt in your mouth," I said.

"Dr. Atkins said I can have all the beef I want, so I think I'll have three or four burgers before I try to figure out what to eat for dessert," Yeoman announced.

"Hey, I bet if we were to take your blood type right now, it would be Rocky Road," JP joked.

"I thought we said no more diet jokes," Yeoman snapped back.

"You're the one that keeps talking about Dr. Atkins," JP said in self-defense.

Both were interrupted when the first burger hit the grill with a sizzling sound and an aroma that separated the two friends. Yeoman then turned and went back into The Shed.

JP pulled up a white plastic lawn chair next to the pit and announced, "Hey, Yo-Man, since you're up, when you come back, bring us a beer."

Big, tall Brian strolled up to help me place the remaining

morsels of meat on the grill and said, "I never get tired of eating mesquite-cooked meat. Sure beats our hickory wood we normally cook with."

Yeoman, looking for sympathy, said, "Brian, tell JP and Delmar to get off the fat jokes, would you?"

"No problem, Yeoman. I'll just hit JP on top of the head so hard it will sprain his ankles," Brian said.

Brian was so much taller than anyone else at The Shed, he probably could have done just that. These were the reasons we gathered at The Shed in the first place—cooking meat, snacking on Redneck Caviar, telling jokes and hunting and fishing stories, and drinking beer.

"Do you think we'll have good food in Texas when we go deer hunting in January?" Yeoman asked.

JP quickly answered, "The cook, Mr. Roy, used to be Queen Elizabeth's and Princess Diana's Mexican cook, or so they say. It says on their website that Mr. Roy cooks brisket with every meal."

"Well, if that's true, then it's no wonder Princess Diana was so skinny. She must have always had the squirts from all the brisket Mr. Roy cooked for breakfast, lunch, and dinner,"

Brian said.

We ate every hamburger, along with all the Redneck Caviar. We were just about to open a second case of beer when JP yelled, "I need help cleaning up the dishes! Don't everyone jump up at one time." JP opened a fresh Miller Lite, left the kitchen, and pulled up a chair around the fire pit. "Let's talk about January's deer hunt. I didn't want to fool with the damn dishes anyway. I was just trying to be neighborly."

Everyone grabbed the white plastic chairs Bonnie had bought from Walmart and sat around the same fire pit that just cooked forty-two huge hamburgers.

"All right, here's the deal. I'm going to shoot the biggest buck that has ever been shot in the state of Texas," Yeoman explained.

"Yeoman, if you saw the biggest buck in Texas, you'd just wet your pants," Brian chuckled.

"Yeah, right. When it comes to deer hunting, I'm the toughest, most vicious hunter alive," said Yeoman. "Why, I've even killed a deer with my bare hands and a knife."

Everyone around the fire laughed uncontrollably.

Yeoman, now with a red face, said, "Let me tell you the story before you guys bust a gut."

"Please do, Yo-Man. But before you do, let me get a fresh beer. All right, everyone, quiet down and let's listen to the great hunter," I said, opening my last beer of the evening.

"I was hunting down off Highway 64, right at the river that separates Davie County and Davidson County," Yeoman explained. "There were about 650 acres of prime deer hunting that had lots of tall, big oak trees to put stands in."

"Like you could get your big butt in a tree stand," laughed JP.

"Hey, this was about thirty years and 150 pounds ago, JP," snapped Yeoman. "Well, anyway, as I was saying, I was hunting out of a stand in a tall white oak tree when, all of a sudden, a pain hit me. I had to pee and pee right then. So I quickly climbed out of my stand with my gun over my shoulder, and to the bottom of the tree I went. Just as soon as I hit the ground and started peeing, I heard a limb crack about fifty yards behind me, toward the river."

Everyone was on the edge of their seats, waiting for Yeoman to get to what we thought was the punch line.

"It was a deer, a buck, that looked to be an eight-pointer," explained Yeoman. "I slowly raised my gun and shot this deer just behind the shoulder, where I knew that it would be a quick kill. After I shot, the deer kicked up his back legs and ran out of sight over the hill toward the river bottom. When I finished peeing, it began to rain a hard and steady cold rain."

"You said you killed the deer with your knife. I knew this was just another one of your stories," interrupted Brian.

"If you'll shut up, I'll finish telling you the rest of the hunt, Brian," said Yeoman. "I leaned my gun on the oak tree and went looking for the buck's blood trail. First, there was a lot of blood and he was easy to trail, but then as it rained harder the trail went away, so I was just blindly looking for what I knew had to be a dead deer by now. Then, all of a sudden, I saw the buck lying in a thicket with his head slightly raised. *Not quite dead yet*, I thought. Figuring it was almost dead, I thought I would just sneak up behind the deer, jump on his back, and slit his throat."

Now, everyone was laughing, just imagining Yeoman on the back of a wounded, yet alive, buck.

"The plan was working perfectly, and I slipped through

the wet leaves within two feet of this wounded deer. Then I pounced like a wild man onto this deer's back with my knife ready to strike, when, all of a sudden, he jumped up and started running around in circles with me on his back." Yeoman spoke more excitedly now. "This deer, with me on his back, ran through every thicket and briar patch on the river bottom. I stabbed that deer while I was getting the hell beat out of me by trees and briars. Finally, victory. The deer slowly lay down and died in the muddy river bottom with me still on his back. My deer and I just lay there while I tried my best to breathe and recover from the worst beating of my life. The rain was coming down harder when I wrapped my belt around the buck's antlers for the long drag out of the woods and into the back of my truck. Now, here's the best part. As I was dragging that deer out of the woods, I saw another buck lying at the edge of a pine thicket. As I got closer, I realized that this second deer was actually the one I shot, and the one I was dragging was not wounded at all."

Brian spit beer into the fire to keep from choking, and Mike and the rest of the guys cracked up. Yeoman knew he had suckered us and laughed uncontrollably. All of a sudden, we heard a loud crack. Pieces of white plastic chair went flying through the air, and Yeoman's head just missed the front of the tractor as he hit the ground and rolled down the hill by the fire pit. Everyone ran to Yeoman's side to make sure he was okay. We gathered around and helped him up.

Yeoman was still laughing when he got to his feet, announced to everyone he was okay, and said, "What a great way to end the night."

I agreed, as we were all out of beer anyway.

As all my hunting buddies and I slowly staggered to The Shed, Delmar said, "Damn, Yo-Man, when I saw all this plastic flying, I just knew you'd be farting milk jugs for the next couple of weeks. Glad you're okay, buddy."